GHOST
SOULLESS KINGS MC: MARBLE FALLS, TX
BOOK 3

ANDI RHODES

BLUE JOURNEY PUBLISHING

Copyright © 2025 by Andi Rhodes

All rights reserved.

No part of this book may be reproduced in any form or by any electronic or mechanical means, including information storage and retrieval systems, without written permission from the author, except for the use of brief quotations in a book review.

This is a work of fiction and the product of the author's imagination. All names, characters, businesses, places, events and incidents are used in a fictitious manner, unless otherwise noted. Any resemblance to actual persons, living or deceased, or actual events is purely coincidental.

Cover Artwork - © Dez Purington at Pretty in Ink Creations

Editing - Darcie Fisher at Into the Gray Author Services

A NOTE FROM THE AUTHOR:

Welcome back to the world of the Soulless Kings MC: Marble Falls, TX chapter! You're about to read Ghost and Ember's story, and I'm not gonna lie, it's an emotional ride. If you're familiar with my work, you know I don't shy away from topics that can be triggering, and normally, I don't want to spoil things, but I don't feel this to be a spoiler.

It's no secret that Ghost transferred into the Marble Falls chapter after patching in as a brother of the Oregon chapter. He did this after learning that his mother has Alzheimer's, and he wanted to be closer to her. That being said, that particular part of his story can, at times, be heart-wrenching. I suggest a box of tissues and a bottle of wine.

I have drawn from personal experience with my own grandmother's Alzheimer's, as well as research on the disease. I would not wish it on anyone, not even my worst enemy (I'd rather give them the uncontrollable shits when they're miles and miles from the nearest bathroom💩), as it is horribly debilitating for both patient and family/friends. Please remember, though, at the end of the day, this is still a work of fiction, and I do take creative liberties to tell the story that Ghost and Ember needed told.

I hope like hell that you love these two (and Mrs. West) as much as I do!

Much love,
    Andi

"The most fucked up joke the universe will play on you is letting you meet the right person at the wrong time."
-Unknown

"And sometimes, the universe will right the wrong and give you that person all over again at the exact right time."
-Andi Rhodes

Ghost...

Marble Falls, Texas is where I grew up, but I left to chase my dreams. Unfortunately, my fiancée didn't follow me to Oregon, and the relationship failed. When my dream became a nightmare, the Soulless Kings MC became my family, and now, more than ever, they're my life.

Family obligations brought me back to Texas, and I wouldn't have it any other way. With my mom barely recognizing me most of the time, my chosen brothers are all I have. But I can't keep up with her care on my own, so I hire the one person I trust with my mom even if it means risking my sanity.

Ember...

I've always wanted to be a nurse, and caring for the elderly is a passion of mine. My life's mission is to provide comfort to those whose family has abandoned them in their time of need. I'm good at what I do and count myself lucky to be able to do it.

Then *he* hires me to care for his mom, and as much as I want to turn down the job, I can't. There was a time his family would've been my own, but life had other plans. Now that we're in each other's lives again, I'm not sure I'll be strong enough to walk away again when the time comes.

Dreams tore them apart, life brought them back together, and danger lurks in the shadows. Can Ghost and Ember survive the storm, let alone each other?

PROLOGUE
EMBER

I can't do this.

Fifteen years ago...

"I have to do this."

I swipe at the tears sliding down my cheeks, but it's useless. They're never going to stop. As long as Parker sticks to his stupid life plan, crying is all I have left.

"What about me?" I ask for the millionth time.

He closes the distance between us and pulls me against his chest. "This was always the plan, Em. You knew I'd be leaving as soon as I graduated from the academy."

"But Oregon? Why can't you stay in Marble Falls and be a cop?"

He sighs and rests his chin on my head. "Because

Marble Falls isn't exactly a hub of activity. I wanna be in the action, work my way to the top. You know that."

Yeah, but I thought marrying me would be enough to keep him here.

Anger rises to the surface, but I temper it down. If the tears aren't working, fury sure as hell won't. Pushing out of his arms, I take several steps back.

"How are we supposed to make a marriage work when we're in two different states?"

Parker rests his hands on his hips. "Seriously? I thought you'd be coming with me."

"And drop out of school?" I shake my head. "I don't think so."

"There are schools in Oregon," he says, exasperation in his tone. "You can finish your nursing degree there, can't you?"

"Yeah, but…"

"But what?" he presses.

I take a deep breath and force the words out. "You've never even asked me to come with you."

"We're engaged!" Parker explodes. "I didn't think I had to ask my fiancé to move with me. I assum—"

"There," I shout, pointing at him. "That right there is the problem. You assumed, but you never asked."

Disbelief registers in his eyes, and I get it… sort

of. We've been together since high school so marriage, babies, a white picket fence, and two point five kids was always the plan, a foregone conclusion.

Hell, he proposed to me the day after graduation. I want to spend my life with him, but I want that life to be here, in Marble Falls.

"What do you want from me?" he asks, his voice cutting through the tension like a hot knife through butter.

My lungs constrict at his question, and breathing becomes almost impossible. Parker has been my life for as long as I can remember, and the thought of existing without him is almost as unbearable as it gets.

Almost.

"I-I-I…" I stutter and shake my head as if it will make what I'm about to do easier somehow. "I can't do this."

His shoulders stiffen. "Do what, Em?"

I lift my eyes to his, and the pain reflected in the brown orbs lashes at my heart like a whip.

"Em?" he prods.

"I can't marry you."

CHAPTER 1
GHOST

And… she's gone.

Present day…

"What the fuck are you doing?"

I slow my steps and turn around to face Crow, my president, and the tension in my body intensifies almost painfully. He's wearing a scowl that no doubt matches my own but for a very different reason.

"What does it look like?" I snap, momentarily having a lapse in judgment and forgetting who I'm talking to.

He narrows his eyes. "Excuse me?"

Heaving a sigh, I force my posture to relax. "Sorry, Pres. I, uh…" I scrub my hands down my face. "Another one quit."

Immediately, his anger deflates. "Jesus, I'm sorry. That makes what, four?"

I huff out a humorless laugh. "Five."

"Have you talked to Addison?" he asks.

Addison is Crow's old lady, and she's also a cop with deeper community ties than Soulless Kings MC. He's been telling me for months to ask her if she knows any home health nurses that would be good for my mom.

"Haven't had the chance."

"Look, go do what you have to do," he orders. "You've got a pass on church. But dammit, talk to Addison when you get back. She can help."

"Thanks, man. I owe you one."

"You don't owe me shit," he scoffs. "But next time you have to bail on church because of something to do with your mom, let someone know."

"Yeah, okay." I turn to walk out the clubhouse door but glance over my shoulder. "Crow?"

"Huh?"

"Thanks. I mean it."

He nods once and spins on his heel. I continue outside to my Harley, mentally preparing myself for what I know is going to be a rough interaction.

As I ride across town, I let my mind wander.

Excitement buzzes through my system as I climb the concrete steps to a porch I've missed since I've been in

Oregon. It's been almost a year since my last visit, and I miss my mom. Her neighbor called me a week ago to tell me she was worried about her, so I made the trek for a visit.

"Mom!" I call out after stepping into my childhood home, a wave of nostalgia washing over me. "Hey, Mom!"

The living room is empty, so I make my way to the kitchen, knowing that's where she has to be with as much as she loves to bake. When I find it empty as well, my stomach knots, and I search faster.

"Mom? Where are you?"

I start to turn toward the hallway when movement outside the kitchen window catches my eye. My mom is standing in the yard, her back to the house, and her shoulders hunched.

"Hey, Mom," I say when I step through the sliding glass door that sits right off the kitchen. "I've been looking for you."

Slowly, she turns around, and my stomach bottoms out. She's got dark circles under her eyes, and her skin is pale.

"Pete?" she asks, calling me by my dad's name… my dead dad.

I shake my head. "C'mon, Mom. That's not funny."

Her stare remains on me for the span of a heartbeat, and then she straightens with a smile. "Parker!" Mom hurries toward me, her arms wide for a hug. "What are you doing here?"

The lump in my throat makes it impossible to answer so I simply wrap her in my arms and kiss the top of her head. When she steps back, I could almost convince myself that I imagined the last few minutes.

As I turn onto the street I grew up on, I give myself a mental shake. Holding onto memories—good or bad—has never done me any favors. Pulling into the driveway, a sense of dread washes over me. If Mom is having a bad enough day that the nurse quit, this isn't going to be pretty.

After parking, I head inside, bracing myself for what's to come. As soon as I cross the threshold, fury slams through me like a Mack truck. The living room is in shambles. I take in the scene, narrowing my eyes on the broken lamp and shattered picture frames before my gaze lands on a sight that will forever be emblazoned on my brain: my mom cowered in the corner like a child.

Jesus.

As slowly as I can, I cross the room and squat in front of her. It takes her a moment to realize she's not alone, and when she does, her eyes widen in fear.

"Who are you?" she asks, her voice frighteningly tiny.

"Hi, Mom," I say quietly. "It's me, Parker."

She shakes her head and then glances around frantically. "Where's my son? I want my son."

I try to reach for her hands, but she yanks them away. Sighing, mentally count to five. "I'm your son, Mom. Remember?"

"She wanted me to leave. I didn't want to leave."

"Who, Mom?"

Since returning to Marble Falls after my mom's Alzheimer's diagnosis, I've learned a few things. For example, if I repeatedly call her 'mom', even when she doesn't recognize me, the repetition may trigger her mind to remember. So, I say it every chance I get.

"That horrible woman. I told her I had to stay here until my boy gets home from school, but she wouldn't listen."

"I'm sorry, Mom. But I'm here."

Her eyes find mine, and I can tell the second clarity returns. Her fear diminishes, and she smiles. "Parker, what are you doing here?" She scans the room. "What happened here? It's a mess."

I rise to my full height and reach out a hand to help her to her feet. "You don't remember what happened?"

"Of course, I know what happened?" she snaps. "You and your friends made a mess. I suggest you clean it up if you still want to go to that dance this weekend."

And… she's gone.

CHAPTER 2
EMBER

What. The. Hell?

"Why don't you go home?"

I shake my head, ignoring the tears that threaten to spill out onto my cheeks. As a home health nurse specializing in caring for the elderly, I'm no stranger to death and dying, but that doesn't mean it's easy. My patients are everything to me, and I'd been with Mrs. Franklin longer than most.

"I'm fine," I insist, not looking at Harold. As the mortician, he and I have stood over numerous bodies together, and he's always trying to look out for me. "I'm all she had, and Mrs. Franklin deserves to not be left alone."

He gives a curt nod, refocusing on preparing the

body to be transported to the funeral home. "Usual arrangements?"

Harold and I have an agreement. He gets my business, and I get a discount. "Yeah."

"Okay. I'll call you when everything's ready."

"Thanks."

It's another twenty minutes before Harold leaves with Mrs. Franklin safely tucked away in the back of the hearse. I'm exhausted all the way to my soul, but I still have to go home and submit the forms required by my agency when we lose a patient.

The drive home is a somber one. I think about those I've lost, the ones who no longer had family or friends to give a rat's ass when they were gone. It breaks my heart knowing that so many people don't have anyone to love them.

They have you.

And I'm not so naive as to think that I'm enough. I've never been enough, especially when it mattered most. But I'm all they have, and I know I bring them some measure of comfort.

Dusk is just settling in when I reach my house, and I take a moment to appreciate the stillness in the air. I live in the country, and I'm never more grateful for it than when I'm coming home after a loss.

"You chose this career," I whisper to myself. "You make a difference."

As soon as I'm inside, I kick off my sensible shoes and toss my purse onto the entry table. It's been two days since I've been home, having chosen to remain by Mrs. Franklin's side at the end. I need a shower, comfy clothes, and food before I can even think about paperwork.

Before heading to the bathroom, I grab the half-full bottle of wine from the fridge, not bothering with a glass, and pop the cork. I swallow a large sip as I trudge down the hall.

The hot water of the shower soothes my aching muscles but does little to ease the ache in my heart. When I became a nurse, I worked primarily in a hospital setting, but it didn't take me long to recognize that secondary trauma is real, and I wanted none of it.

I've had enough trauma of my own to last two lifetimes.

Once I'm clean, I wrap myself in a fluffy blue towel and take another healthy swig of my wine. I change into a pair of baggy sweats and an oversized tee before slipping my feet into my slippers and returning to the kitchen.

My fridge is full of takeout containers, and since I can't remember when I ordered them, I close the door and move to the pantry. Grabbing a bag of Nacho Cheese Doritos, I rip it open and shove one into my mouth.

I make a mental note to go grocery shopping tomorrow as I walk to my office. When I step inside, I scan the shelves on the wall, acknowledging those who went before Mrs. Franklin.

"You'll all like her," I say to the urns. "She was sweet."

"Here, let me help you."

I take a step back from the shelf in the cookie aisle and smile at the teenage grocery clerk.

"Thanks."

He hands me the package of Double Stuffed Oreos, and I toss it into my cart with all the other junk food. I should've made a list before I left the house, but I have to go into the office to read up on the new patient I'll be assigned now that Mrs. Franklin is gone.

And before you judge me, there's some fruits and veggies along with the junk food. I'm a nurse, after all.

A half-hour later, I'm making my way to the

checkout when I hear my name being called. I turn around and smile.

"Hey, Addison," I greet. "Long time, no see."

Addison and I don't run in the same circles—hell, I don't run in any circles… I'm a homebody when I'm not working—but it's not unheard of for us to cross paths in our lines of work, especially when I'm dealing with unruly family members of patients.

"I heard about Mrs. Franklin," she says.

"Yeah, that was a tough one," I admit.

"She was lucky to have you."

"Thanks."

"Listen, I'm glad I ran into you." She glances around as if to make sure we can't be overheard. "I was going to call you later, and this saves me from having to do that."

My skin prickles with unease. Why would she need to call me? I no longer have a reason for police to be involved in my life now that my parents are dead, and I can't think of anything I've done wrong so—

"Wipe that look off your face," she admonishes. "It's nothing bad."

I breathe a sigh of relief. "Oh. Okay."

"I've got a job for you."

"Um… Have you filled out the form with the agency?"

She shakes her head. "This would be an off the books job." When I stare at her with confusion, she continues. "One of Crow's MC brothers needs a nurse for his mom. He asked if I could help him with that, and I immediately thought of you."

I'd heard something about Addison marrying a biker. It was hard to miss that info because the gossip spread like wildfire in our small town.

Interesting choice as the police chief's daughter, but to each their own.

"Do you have any specifics about the patient?" I ask, curious.

She scrunches her nose. "Some. But I can have the son give you a call later if that's okay. He'd be better to talk to about it."

"Okay. Sounds good."

"Oh, and heads up," she says. "His mom needs a full-time nurse who can be with her twenty-four-seven. You'd be compensated appropriately, of course." She reaches into her pocket, pulls out her cell, and hands it to me. "Here, put your cell number in there so I can pass it along."

I do as she says as I try to process the conversation. As soon as I return her phone to her, she smiles and says to expect a call later, and then she's gone.

What. The. Hell?

CHAPTER 3
GHOST

Or at least I used to.

"I'm getting bored."

I smirk at Poker, the club's Enforcer, and shake my head. We've been in the Nightmare Room with Sonny, a low-level drug dealer who somehow got his hands on our product and thought it would be okay to sell it for his own profit. Fucking idiot.

"Where'd you get the powder?" I demand, shifting my attention back to Sonny.

"I told you," the prick sneers like he's not about to lose his life any second. "I work for Limitless Throttle."

I haul my fist back and crack him in the nose for the tenth time. "Ya know, I might stop doing that if you'd tell the fucking truth."

Soulless Kings MC and Limitless Throttle MC haven't been enemies for a while, not since Shuffle became president. Hell, they even helped us eradicate the Wingless Angels.

Sonny spits blood onto the concrete floor as his body sways from the chains hanging him from the ceiling.

"Dude, he's goin' easy on you," Poker tells him, his bored expression morphing into a sinister grin as he stalks toward the man. "I won't be so nice."

For a piece of shit dealer, Sonny's got balls, I'll give him that. Normally, this would be the point where our captive is begging for mercy, not tempting the devil.

"Gimme whatever you got," Sonny taunts. "I can take it."

Poker and I exchange a look before he walks to the wall and snags the fire poker from its perch. Next, he grabs the torch and hands it to me.

"Make it glow," he snarls.

I open the fuel valve, and a blue flame shoots out of the nozzle. Poker sticks the tip of the iron into the heat, and both of us stare at Sonny for several minutes while we let the tool get hot.

"W-what are you doing?" Sonny asks, fear finally entering his voice.

Poker walks toward him, the glowing tip of the

stoker a promise of what's to come. When he reaches the swaying man, he taunts him by holding the fire poker centimeters from his skin, careful not to touch him.

"We gave you every opportunity to tell us what we want to hear," our enforcer says with a shrug. "You chose not to."

He shoves the tip into Sonny's thigh, and the man screams like a little girl. Having been a cop, you'd think I'd detest stuff like this, but I don't. There's something about not having to worry about blurred lines that just feels… right.

"O-okay, I'll tell you."

"Seriously?" I drawl. "That's all you can take?" I glance at Poker. "Didn't he just tell us to give him all we got, brother?"

"He did."

"Whaddya say we up our game?"

Poker stretches his arm toward me so I can light up the tip of the implement again. Once it glows orange, he faces Sonny and shoves the heated spike into his chest, right where the prick's heart lies beneath the ribs.

"Dammit, man," I groan when Sonny's head lolls to the side, his eyes vacant of any sign of life. "You killed him."

"I didn't mean to."

"Bullshit," I retort with a dark chuckle. "If you meant to keep him breathing, you'd have aimed lower."

"Eh, who cares? He was a waste of breath anyway."

"Yeah, and you're gonna be the one to fucking tell Crow. He wanted answers, and we got nothing."

"And we weren't gonna get anything," he snaps, tossing the fire poker to the cement floor.

He flattens his palm on the scanner by the door, and the steel barrier slides open. Poker stalks out of the Nightmare Room. As I follow him down the hall to the stairs, my phone vibrates in my pocket. I pull it out and stare at the text.

> Crow: Addi got you what you need

Included in the text is a contact sheet for 'Nurse for Ghost'. Fucker couldn't even put a real name in there. I chuckle even as a sense of calm washes over me. If the nurse is someone Addison found, I might actually be able to relax a bit where my mom is concerned.

When Poker and I reach the common room of the clubhouse, he veers off to speak to Crow, but I head straight for my suite. I want to place my call immediately, but I need to take a shower first. The blood on my clothes and body isn't going to wash itself off.

Once I'm clean and dressed in a pair of gray sweats, I flop onto my bed, cell phone in hand. I tap the screen a few times, bringing up the contact Crow sent, and then put the call on speakerphone while I wait for an answer.

The feminine voice that comes through the line is muffled. "Hello."

"Hi, um, I got your number from Addison," I say.

A sharp intake of breath is my only response. I wait for several seconds, hoping the woman will say something, but she doesn't.

"This is the nurse who knows Addison Thompson?" I pause. "Or maybe you know her as Addison McGill, the cop."

She clears her throat but still doesn't speak.

"Look, if you're not interested in the job, then just say so," I snap, annoyed at having my time wasted. "I can find someone else."

"Omigod," the woman groans, so quietly I almost don't hear it. "Is… Is this… Parker?"

That voice. I know it. I know the woman it belongs to better than I know myself.

Or at least I used to.

CHAPTER 4
EMBER

That's the million-dollar question.

Regret barrels into me like a freight train. I shouldn't have answered the call, but now that I have, I'm stuck. Sure, I could hang up and pretend that my world didn't just shift on its axis, and that would make me a coward… Which I'm not.

Sure feels like you are.

I glance at the TV where Dean Winchester is frozen with his mouth open on a scream. This is my favorite episode of *Supernatural*, and I wish I would've kept watching instead of pausing it.

"Is… Is this… Parker?"

My voice sounds tiny, and I silently berate myself for it.

The man on the other end of the call swears under his breath. "Em?"

The way my shortened name rolls off his tongue sends shivers down my spine, shivers I thought I lost fifteen years ago.

"You're the friend Addi wanted a nurse for?" I ask, trying to wrap my head around what's happening.

"And you're the nurse," he replies, resignation in his tone.

I take a deep breath, then another and another. How had I not put two and two together when I ran into Addison? I've known for a while now that Parker was back in town, but it never occurred to me that *he'd* be the potential new client.

Not Parker… his mother.

My stomach twists as realization dawns. Mrs. West was always one of my favorite people growing up, and it makes me physically ill to know she's sick.

"Em? Are you still there?" Parker asks, pulling me from my thoughts.

"Uh, yeah. So…" I swallow past the lump in my throat. "How've you been?"

"How have I been?" he bellows, his voice rougher than I remember. "That's all you have to say to me?"

Anger surges in my blood. "You called me, remember?"

"I didn't know I was calling you!" he shouts. "If I had, I'd have…"

"You'd have what?" I demand when he fails to continue. "Run to another state?"

"That's not fair. Don't make this about what happened between us."

"What else would it be about?"

"Ya know what? Forget it. I'll find someone else."

Parker always did have a penchant for shutting down when things got tough. "Parker, wait," I blurt before I can second-guess myself. "Addison said your mom's in need of a full-time nurse."

He sighs as if the weight of the world is on his shoulders, and I can picture him running his fingers through his chestnut hair, tugging on the ends in frustration.

"It's getting bad, Em," he admits.

I steel myself against the pain in his voice. I've suffered enough because of this man, and I refuse to go down that road again. But…

"Tell me what's going on," I say quietly, knowing in my heart of hearts I might regret it.

Again, he sighs.

Fuck, that sigh.

"She's got Alzheimer's."

And if I thought this conversation was hard

before, I was wrong. Those three words turned hard into gut-wrenching.

"I'm so sorry," I whisper, trying like hell to keep the tears at bay. Mrs. West was—is, dammit, is—such a sweet woman, and the thought of her losing herself to a merciless disease tears a hole in my already ragged soul.

"Thanks. But it's not an apology I need," he says, his tone hardening. "She's run off five nurses already, and I can't let there be a sixth."

"Five?"

"Yeah. And since she needs someone now, I'm back to what I said before… Forget I called. I'll find someone else."

Jesus, he's the most stubborn man I've ever met.

"I'll do it," I blurt before he can hang up on me.

Damn, Ember, you're a glutton for punishment.

"What?"

Now it's my turn to sigh. "You heard me, Parker," I bite out, needing to get some composure over myself, especially if I'm going to be heading straight into the lion's den. "I'll do it."

"You'll have to move in with her. She can't be alone… ever."

"Okay. I-I can do that."

"Don't you have a husband or boyfriend or something who'll have a problem with this?"

I huff out a laugh. "Not that it's any of your business, but no, I don't. Don't you have a wife or girlfriend or something who'll have a problem with your ex living with your mother?" I counter cooly.

"Old lady."

"What?"

"I'm a biker, so it's old lady."

"And that matters because?"

"Oh, it matters," he says, his tone turning raspy. "Not that it's any of your business, but no, I don't have anyone who will give a shit."

"Okaaay. Well, now that we've established that…" I clear my throat. "When do you want me to start?"

"Seriously? You don't want to go over the pay or anything like that?"

I'd do it for free, but he doesn't need to know that.

"Right. Um… Can you meet in the morning for coffee? We can go over the particulars then."

"You're really gonna do this?" he asks, disbelief dripping from his words.

"Yeah, I guess I am."

"Why?"

Ding, ding, ding. That's the million-dollar question.

"Because Parker. It's your mom."

CHAPTER 5
GHOST

I DON'T WANT HER SYMPATHY.

BECAUSE PARKER. IT'S YOUR MOM.

I stare at my phone in disbelief. After that statement, Ember and I agreed on a time and place to meet in the morning and ended our call. When I dialed the number Crow gave me, I had no idea that my past was going to rear its ugly head and haunt me.

It took years for me to get over Ember, or so I thought. Hearing her voice sent a zing through my system I haven't experienced since… well, since her. Hiring her to care for my mom is a horrible idea, and after a restless night, I talk myself out of doing just that.

The ride to the coffee shop seems to last a lifetime,

and by the time I arrive, I feel confident in my decision. After parking next to the curb in front of the building, I stride toward the door, and my heart stops when my eyes land on Ember through the glass.

Holy fuck!

I've spent years telling myself that time will have been bad for my ex-fiancée, but shit, was I wrong. Her curly red hair is still as glossy as it was the last time I saw her, and her ass is as perfect now as it was back then. It's an ass I'd recognize anywhere.

As if magnetically tethered to me, she glances over her shoulder, and her blue eyes bore into me. Those eyes narrow for a split-second before she forces a smile. I take a deep breath and pull open the door, breaking the last barrier between us.

"Parker," she greets when I reach her at the counter.

"Hi, Em."

"What can I get ya?" the barista asks.

After we both have our orders, Ember and I move through the small café to a table in the corner. Before she can take the seat giving her a view of the door, I slide into the booth. She stares at me for a moment and then shakes her head.

"Some things never change," she mutters.

Inwardly, I wince because I *have* changed… a lot.

But, yeah, some things will always be the same, and my need to have full awareness of my surroundings is one of those things.

"So," I say.

"So," she repeats.

"How have you been?"

Ember huffs out a breath. "Seriously?"

"What?"

"We haven't spoken in fifteen years, and that's your opener?"

"Seems like a good place to start." I shrug. "What would you prefer?"

She lifts her paper cup to her lips and blows on the steaming hot liquid before taking a careful sip. Her eyes practically roll back into her head as she swallows.

What I wouldn't give to have her look like that while she swallows me *down.*

My cock stiffens behind my fly, and I squirm in an effort to adjust myself. If she notices, she says nothing, thank fuck.

"Look, this meeting isn't about us or how we've been," she begins, straightening in her seat. "I think we're both adult enough to keep things professional."

"Is that what you want?" I ask without thinking.

"Parker, this isn't about what I want, it's about

what you need." Her throat bobs. "What your mom needs, I mean."

I smirk. I'm affecting her, and I find that I'm thrilled with that fact. "Right. Well, like I said last night, she needs full-time care."

"And you can't provide that?"

I shake my head. "I'm at the house as much as I can be."

"Which is how often?"

There's the tiniest hint of judgment in her tone, but I choose to ignore it. "A few times a week," I admit.

A wrinkle appears across her forehead as she digests that information. "What could possibly be more—" Ember presses her lips together. "Ya know what? Never mind. What exactly is it that you want from me?"

"I think that's pretty clear."

"Parker, with you, nothing is clear." She leans back and crosses her arms over her chest. The off-the-shoulder sweater she's wearing drops a little lower, and my mouth waters at the sight of a tattoo that wasn't there years ago. "I need you to spell it out for me."

Taking a deep breath, I rest my elbows on the table. "Mom has good days and bad, which I'm learning is normal at this stage of the disease. But her

Alzheimer's is progressing, and the bad days are becoming more frequent. I need a nurse who can live with her full-time, manage her medications, help her with any and all tasks that require assistance, and I need someone who knows how to handle situations as they arise."

"Situations?"

"Em, all of her nurses have quit because my mom has been… *difficult*."

"In other words, she's a fairly typical Alzheimer's patient."

"If you say so."

Ember sighs, and her shoulders slump. "I can't imagine how hard this is for you."

The unexpected sympathy sets my teeth on edge. I don't want her sympathy. In fact, I've let this little meeting go on way too long as it is. I came here resolved not to follow through with hiring Ember, yet I still sit here talking to her like I will.

"I should go," I say, sliding out of the booth and getting to my feet. "I'll find someone to take care of my mom, but it can't be you."

With those parting words, I stride out of the café, tossing my coffee into the trash as I pass it. Every part of me wants to look back at the woman I thought I'd share my life with, but I don't. It would only end badly.

CHAPTER 6
EMBER

That is the question, isn't it?

The rumble of Parker's Harley as he fires it up pulls me from my stupor. One minute, we're talking, and it feels like we're getting somewhere, and the next, he shuts down. I thought I knew Parker, but apparently, I knew the boy and not the man.

He is definitely all man.

I remain in my seat, replaying the conversation with him in my head. As much as I want to let it go, forget we ever spoke again, I can't. His mom needs help, and I can give that to her.

Yes, that's it. If I take the job, it's for Mrs. West, not Parker.

I dig through my purse for my cell, determined to see this through. When my fingers curl around the device, I pull it out and open my texting app to send a message to him.

> Me: I'll take the job. But I have conditions. I'll be at the coffee shop for another half hour. Come back and we'll talk. Or don't. Up to you.

While I wait to see what he'll do, I return to the counter and order another coffee and blueberry muffin. Might as well eat. Twenty minutes pass, then another five, and I'm about to leave when Parker slips back into the booth across from me.

"I wasn't sure you'd come back," I admit.

"Neither was I." He tilts his head. "What are your conditions?"

"Um…" I lick my lips. "Well, I can't do twenty-four-seven. Even live-in nurses need a break."

"That won't work. I told you, she ne—"

"Full-time care," I snap, holding a hand up. "Yeah, I know. But I bet you can be at the house at least one day a week. Surely, the club can spare you for that long."

His eye twitches at the corner, a tell that he's annoyed. "How'd you know about the club?"

Either he's lost some brain cells over the years or he's as distracted by me as I am him.

I nod toward him. "Well, that vest is a dead give-away. And there's also the fact that I know Addison is married to the Soulless Kings president, and she said it was a brother who needed help."

Parker glances down at his vest, and when he locks his gaze with mine again, he's smirking. "Cut."

"Excuse me?"

"It's a cut, not a vest."

"Oh, well… okay."

"I'm surprised you didn't comment on it earlier."

I shrug. "Wasn't what we needed to talk about."

"True." I fold my hands on top of the table. "So, is that something you can do? Can you give me one day off a week?"

"I think I can manage that, unless club business comes up."

"Parker, this isn't a negotiation," I say, forcing a business-like tone. "Either you agree, or I walk."

"Call me Ghost," he says, pointing to the patch on his vest—no, cut. "And everything is a negotiation, Em."

I shake my head. "No, it—"

"I can give you at least one day a week, but I need to know that if something comes up, you'll be flexible about the day. And when I can, I'll give you a full two days. I don't expect you to work yourself to death."

"Okay. I can live with that."

"Next one," he prompts.

"Next one what?"

The corner of his mouth tips up. "Condition. Your text suggested there was more than one."

"Oh, right. I'm guessing that, other than the Alzheimer's, your mom is healthy."

"She is," he confirms.

"Then I'll likely be living with her for a while. The compensation needs to match what I make through the agency since I won't be able to take on more patients. They'll probably have to replace me, depending on the length of this job, so I need to know that you'll provide me with a good reference once it's all over."

"Once Mom dies, you mean?"

Sighing, I nod. "Yeah. I'm sorry, but that's—"

"It's okay, Em. I know that's the only way this arrangement ends."

"This isn't an *arrangement*. It's a job, Parker."

"Ghost," he reminds me.

"Right, Ghost."

"As for the pay, I'll double your current salary, cover your mortgage payments, and provide you with a generous stipend to cover any expenses that are above and beyond what Mom's medical expenses are."

"I… wow." A thought occurs to me, and I narrow

my eyes. "How can you afford that? It's not dirty money, is it?"

His eyes darken, and he scowls. "Do you really think so little of me?"

I have no clue how to answer that, so I settle for the brutal truth. "I don't know you."

He rears back as if I slapped him, and pain flashes in his eyes, but he recovers so quickly that I convince myself I imagined it. "Touché."

"You haven't answered my question," I remind him.

"I'm a single man with very little expenses," he explains. "I've got plenty of money that I earned before I even patched in."

My heart stutters on his admission that he's single. Why, I don't know, but there ya have it. "Okay."

"What about you?" he asks, and when I wrinkle my forehead in confusion, he continues. "Are you single?"

"Does it matter?"

He seems to consider that for a moment before shrugging. "Guess not."

"Look, I want to help. But this isn't going to be a walk down memory lane or anything else related to our past, for that matter," I tell him.

"Didn't think it would be," he mutters.

"Good. Now, my last condition."

"I'm listening," he replies sarcastically.

"I'll be living in your mother's house, but I still have mine. I'm gonna need help with keeping the lawn mowed and anything else that might need done while I'm gone. Can you handle that?"

"Can I handle all the things I should've been doing as your husband had you not broken things off?" he bites out. "Yeah, Em, I think I can fuckin' handle that." He arches a brow. "The question is, can you?"

I swallow past the lump in my throat.

That *is* the question, isn't it?

CHAPTER 7
GHOST

This is gonna be fucking hard as hell, isn't it?

"Better hurry."

I nod at Conner, one of the prospects, as I make my way through the common room of the clubhouse. After I left Ember at the coffee shop, I rode around for a while in an attempt to get my head on straight. I was so caught up in my own shit that I forgot I had to be back for church.

"Sorry," I say as I slide into my chair around the long conference table in the meeting room. "Got sidetracked."

Crow glares at me, but he must see something in my expression because he doesn't comment. Journey, our VP, has no such problem.

"Don't let it fucking happen again," he barks. "And you owe Stunner fifty bucks on your way out," he says, referring to the fine for being late and our treasurer.

"Got it."

"Now that we're all here," Crow begins. "Let's run through our normal business, and then we'll get to the epic shitstorm brewing on the streets." He nods at Stunner to let him know he can present his report.

"The clinic is doing well," Stunner states. "We might treat patients for free, but the donations continue to come in and more than keep it afloat."

"But we could use a second doctor," Jackyl, the club doc, adds. "Hell, even a nurse practitioner would be good."

"Can we do that?" Crow asks Stunner.

The treasurer shrugs. "Don't see why not. We've got the cash flow, and there's certainly enough patients to justify it."

Pres faces Jackyl. "Go ahead and start looking. I'll leave the salary up to you and Stunner."

"Consider it done," Stunner quips, and when no one says another word about the clinic, he continues. "Moving on. Soulless Ink is in the black, as always."

"Damn straight it is," Python says with a grin. "I do good fucking work."

Crow shakes his head. "Yeah, you do," he comments dryly, as if placating a child.

Stunner clears his throat. "I'm wondering if it wouldn't be a good idea to hire another artist to help out. Appointments are up, and with the shit about to hit the fan in other businesses, Python might not be able to devote as much time at SI."

Pres shifts his gaze to the tattooist in question. "You good with that, brother?"

Python narrows his eyes. "You know I don't work well with others."

"I'm sure Ben can attest to that," I say with a chuckle. "Poor prospect comes home after working with you and looks like crawling into Hell would be more fun."

"See," Python snaps. "I ain't takin' anyone else on."

"Not sure you've gotta fuckin' choice in the matter," Crow says hotly. "Would you rather business falls off because people get tired of waiting on your grumpy ass?"

"What about Braydon?" Screamer suggests, referring to our newest prospect. "He's a talented motherfucker with his drawings." Our road captain shrugs. "Maybe you could be his mentor or some shit."

"Dude can draw, that's for sure," Python grudgingly admits. "But can he follow orders?"

"Best to find out at the shop and not during other club business, don't ya think?" Poker states.

Python grumbles unintelligibly. "Yeah, fine. I guess you've gotta point."

"It's settled then," Crow says matter-of-factly. "Take Braydon with you to Soulless Ink tomorrow and see how things go. We can do it on a trial basis, if that makes you feel better."

"A little," Python mumbles.

"And moving on," Journey says as shifts his gaze from one brother to the next. "We've got some shit happening on the streets with our drug sales. We may have eliminated Sonny, but more dealers have popped up, and they're peddling our stuff."

"How the fuck are they getting their hands on it?" Poker demands.

"And what the hell are they lacing it with?" Fudge bites out. "I'm guessing Fentanyl based on the sheer number of deaths, but until we can get our hands on it, we won't know for sure."

"If Poker wouldn't have been in such a damn hurry to waste Sonny, we might have the answers," I snap.

"Gimme a break," Poker argues. "He wasn't gonna give us shit, and you know it."

I shoot to my feet. "No, I don't kn—"

"Sit down!" Crow shouts. "And shut up!"

Obeying my Pres, I plop down into my chair. Poker glares at me so I shift my eyes to Crow.

"Sorry, Pres."

"I get that you've got a lot going on," Crow says. "But don't you dare take it out on us."

"You don't know the half of it," I mutter, leaning back and crossing my arms over my chest.

"Then enlighten us," Journey suggests hotly.

"He can do that after we figure this other shit out," Crow barks. "Right now, we need to know who's killing the people in our town."

"And using our shit to do it," Journey adds.

"Have you talked to Shuffle?" I ask, putting my other worries out of my mind.

Crow thrusts his hand through his hair. "Yeah. He doesn't know shit either. Says he's got all his guys keeping their ears to the ground and will let us know if they hear anything."

"Sounds like we need to set up some stings," I say.

"Careful, Ghost," Screamer says with a chuckle. "The cop in you is showing."

"No, wait." Crow holds his hand up. "I wanna hear more about this."

"Well, Pres, we're getting nowhere right now," I

begin. "I think we need to do a little undercover work, posing as buyers. It's our best shot at finding these fucks."

"It could work," Screamer says.

"Anyone have a better idea?" Crow asks, and everyone remains silent. "Okay, all in favor, thump twice." We all pound the table two times. "Now we just have to figure out which of us will go undercover."

"It was Ghost's idea," Tracer comments, speaking up for the first time. "Clearly, he should go."

Panic blossoms in my chest. "Uh, I ha—"

"I agree with you," Crow says. "But he's got his mother to worry about." My panic eases. "How about Fudge and Tracer, you two take Conner and Jimmy? The four of you should be able to get somewhere, right?"

Tracer groans. "Yeah, we can do that."

"Sure about that?" Journey snaps. "Kinda sounds like you're wanting to argue with Pres."

"Nah, it's just…"

"Just what?"

Tracer shrugs. "I don't know. Doesn't sound all that fun, is all."

"Club business isn't about fun," Crow reminds him. "It's about keeping our place in Marble Falls secure. It's about letting these shit-for-brains know who rules around here."

"You're right."

"Yeah, I know," Crow deadpans before turning to Fudge. "You got a problem with my orders?"

"Nope."

"Good. Then it's settled. I want you two and the prospects to work out a plan within the next forty-eight hours. Report back to me, and we'll go from there."

"You got it," Fudge says.

"Anything else before we close out?" Crow asks, glancing around the table. No one speaks, so he stands. "Dismissed."

My brothers file out of the room, but I hang back. "Hey, Pres, got a minute?"

"Yeah, what's up?"

I rub the back of my neck. "I met with that nurse Addi found."

He grins. "How'd it go?"

"You do realize who she found, right?"

"I'm guessing a damn good nurse."

"I'm sure Ember *is* good," I mutter.

"Wait." Crow holds a hand up. "Ember as in… *the* Ember?"

"How many Embers do you know that live in Marble Falls?" I counter.

"Shit, brother. I didn't know."

"Yeah, well, now you do."

"I'll have Addi try to find some—"

"I already hired her," I blurt.

"You did?"

I nod. "She might be the last person I want to deal with, but she knows my mom, and I'm hoping that will give her an edge."

"Yeah, but…" He sighs. "Are you sure you're up for it? I mean, she practically left you at the altar."

I huff out a humorless laugh. "Not quite."

"Close enough."

"It was a long time ago, and we're both adults. I can handle it."

"Okay, if you're sure."

"I'm not fucking sure of anything," I admit. "But this isn't about me. It's about my mom. I'll do anything for her."

"I know, brother." Crow claps a hand on my shoulder. "Anything I can do to help?"

"One of Em's conditions was that I cover at least one day a week so she can get a break. Will that be a problem?"

"You know it won't. If you need more than that, just let me know."

"Thanks, man. I appreciate it."

"No problem."

I turn to walk away but stop at the door and glance over my shoulder. "This is gonna be fucking hard as hell, isn't it?"

Crow throws his head back and laughs. "I have no doubt."

CHAPTER 8
EMBER

What the hell is he doing here?

"You can't be serious."

I shift in my chair as I maintain eye contact with Janice, my boss, across her desk. When I arrived at the agency this morning to finish up some paperwork, I asked to speak to her in private so I could let her know I'd be leaving for a while. I knew it would be a hard conversation, but I didn't think she'd actually be angry.

"I'm sorry, Janice," I say with a shrug. "This is a patient that I'm uniquely qualified to deal with."

"Your ex-fiancé's mother," she says as if she doesn't quite believe it. "That's a huge conflict of interest."

"Maybe. But she's already gone through several nurses."

"So I've heard."

"What?"

"We're not the only agency in town, and I network," she tells me. "I've heard about the mother of a Soulless King."

I scrunch up my nose. "Right." Living in a small town has its perks, but the rampant gossip isn't one of them. And I find that I'm disappointed that Janice seems to be tapped into that particular grape vine. "Well, I know you can't hold my job," I say, getting to my feet. "Especially since I don't know how long this will be. But I do plan on coming back if there's still a position open."

"You're assuming I'll take you back," she says bluntly.

Masking my frustration, I smile. "Of course."

I've never had a problem with Janice. All of my performance reviews have been stellar, and I care more about the patients than any other employee here. The fact that she's being this petty is pissing me off, especially because it'll be the patients who suffer, not me.

You might suffer. You're gonna be working for Parker —no, Ghost—after all.

"Are you going to work out your notice?" she asks as I turn to leave her office.

I glance over my shoulder. "Do you think that's a good idea? I don't want to start with a new patient only to leave them so soon."

"Right. Fine."

"Look, Janice, I have no problem working out a notice. None at all. I just want what's best for the patients. I hope you know that."

"If that were true, you wouldn't be leaving us," she snaps.

"Ya know what?" I snap back. "No, I won't be working out a notice. I've been a valuable employee for years, and this is how you treat me? I'll make sure all paperwork is completed before I leave but today will be my last day."

I told Ghost I had to give notice and couldn't start for at least two weeks, but I guess I can text him and let him know I can start earlier. Or I could take the time to decompress and get my house ready for me to be gone for who knows how long. Either way, I'm not spending a minute longer in this office than I have to.

Janice nods curtly. "Turn your badge in before you leave."

With that, she returns to whatever she was doing before I came in, effectively dismissing me. I don't know what is going on with her, but she's never treated me so poorly.

Maybe it's her time of the month.

I stifle a laugh and walk to my office. It takes me longer to clear out my personal items than it does to finish up any work, and three hours later, I'm heading to my car. Tears threaten as it finally hits me that a huge chapter of my life is over, but I don't let them fall until I'm safely tucked into the driver's seat.

While I cry, I pull my cell from my purse and type out a quick text.

> Me: I can start any time

Before I can put the car into gear, my cell dings with a notification, and I glance at the screen to see a text from Parker.

I really need to change his contact info if I'm ever going to get used to calling him Ghost like he insists

I do that before I look at the message.

> Ghost: Thought u had to give notice

> Me: I did. Didn't go as planned

> Ghost: Oh. Wanna start tomorrow or do u want a little down time?

> Me: Can you give me 2 days to get things in order at my house?

Ghost: No prob

> Me: Thanks.

I wait for a response, but none comes. Apparently, the matter is settled for him. Rolling my eyes, I put the car in drive and pull out of the parking space in the agency's employee lot. The drive home feels like forever, but I use the time to make a mental list of all the things I need to get done.

When I reach my driveway, a dark figure standing on my porch catches my attention, and I groan when I spot the Harley parked close to the garage door.

Ghost.

What the hell is he doing here?

CHAPTER 9
GHOST

I LOVE THE FUCKING GRAY.

"STALKING IS A CRIME, YA KNOW?"

I smirk at Ember as she walks toward her front porch, a box in her hand that appears to have personal stuff in it. When I left the clubhouse, I had no particular destination in mind. Ending up here was not on the agenda.

Yeah, keep telling yourself that.

An image of her address in my GPS flashes in my mind. "I'm not stalking you," I snap, my annoyance with myself unintentionally directed at Ember.

She arches a perfectly manicured brow. "How'd you know where I live?"

And the answer to that will only confirm her stalker theory.

When I don't respond, she taps her foot. "I'm waiting," she prods.

"Would you believe that I was out for a leisurely ride and just happened upon a house that I thought could be yours?"

She does her best to hide the ghost of a smile threatening, but I know her expressions. The crinkles at the corners of her eyes give her away. "No, Pa—" She presses her lips into a flat line for a split second. "No, *Ghost*, I wouldn't believe it."

I heave a sigh. "Fine. Tracer may or may not have helped me out where your address is concerned."

"Tracer?"

"He's the tech guy for the club."

"He's the hacker, you mean?"

I smirk. "That, too."

Ember shifts the box in her arms as she studies me. Her blue eyes are the same as I remember: full of emotion. Only now, I can't identify the emotion.

"You're different," she finally comments.

"It's been fifteen years, Em."

She rolls her eyes. "No shit," she snaps, pushing past me. She struggles to unlock her door and hold the box at the same time, so I grab the keys from her to help. "Thanks," she mumbles when I push the door open.

"No problem," I reply, following her inside.

"Sure, come on in," Ember says, her tone dripping with sarcasm.

"Thanks. I think I will."

After setting the box on a table by the door, she turns to face me. "What are you doing here?"

I thought about that very thing while I was waiting for her to get home. Hell, I even tried to talk myself into leaving, but clearly, that didn't work.

"I came to offer my services," I finally say.

Her eyes widen. "And what *services* would those be?"

For the first time since I laid eyes on her again, I let my mind wander. My gaze travels from her baby blues to the curve of her shoulder and then down over her chest. Only when I reach the apex of her thighs do they stop. My mouth waters, and I swallow, swearing she can hear the thunk of my Adam's apple.

She clears her throat, jarring me out of my perusal, and I whip my head up to stare at her face.

"Hmm?" I ask, sure I must have missed something she said.

Ember sighs dramatically. "What do you want, Parker?"

"Ghost," I correct automatically.

She waves her hand. "Whatever. What the hell do you want?"

"Honestly?"

"Of course."

"At the moment, I want you," I blurt.

Her hand goes to her throat, and I stifle a groan. "You… Um, you want… me?"

"Sounds crazy, huh?"

Glancing at the box she'd been carrying, she shrugs. "It's been a crazy day."

Hope flares, and I know I should squash it and run out of her house as fast as my size elevens will carry me, but my feet are rooted in place. Nothing good can possibly come from anything happening between us. The problem is, I'm not the honorable man I used to be. I'm not the same person who used to make what I thought were good decisions.

I'm Ghost, a patched member of a one-percenter motorcycle club. I'm a Soulless King who no longer believes in black and white, good and bad. I live and breathe the space in between, the space in the gray.

The moment she levels her gaze back on mine, I'm on her, pushing her back against the wall and fusing my lips to hers.

Like I said… I love the fucking gray.

CHAPTER 10
EMBER

Crazy fucking day.

"Tell me to stop."

Ghost pulls away and looks at me, his eyes pleading for me to do as he asks. I should. I know it, and he knows it. This is a terrible idea. But the second his mouth touched mine, I was lost. And now, I'm fucking desperate.

Rather than respond, I shake my head before tugging him closer by a belt loop. A million reasons flash through my mind as to why I should drag him by said belt loop and toss him out the door, but I force away every single one of them.

I wasn't lying when I said today's been crazy, and this only solidifies it as one for the history books. When Addison approached me in the grocery store, I had no idea how much my life was about to change. I couldn't have known.

Ghost's hand shifts from my hip to slide up my shirt and rest just below my breast. I whimper at the contact, and he smiles against me. Fifteen years… fifteen years and this man can still reduce me to mush.

No! Not going down that road. This is sex, nothing more.

Speaking of sex, I need it. I want it. And he's going to give it to me.

I break away as I start unbuttoning his jeans. "Bedroom's down the hall." He arches a brow, but before he can say anything, I continue. "Don't think. Please, don't think. I don't wanna think."

That's all the encouragement he needs. He lifts me up, and I wrap my legs around his waist. As he carries me down the hall, he kisses me again, his tongue sweeping into my mouth and tangling with mine. Before I know it, he's tossing me onto the bed, and the loss of contact with his body has me moaning.

"Tell me to stop," he repeats, taking his cut off and laying it gently on the top of my dresser. Then he grabs the hem of his shirt at the back of his neck and yanks it over his head.

"No."

"I'm not gonna ask again," he growls, kicking off his boots.

"I thought I told you not to think," I taunt, reaching for the clasp on my dress pants.

With lightning-quick speed, Ghost is on me, stopping my movements. "You know this is my favorite part," he says as he slowly, almost reverently, drags my pants and panties over my hips and down my legs.

It's on the tip of my tongue to tell him I don't know what his favorite part is anymore, but I'm not about to stop the delicious sensations his touch is evoking. Sensations that I haven't felt in too damn long.

My body is on fire, burning from the inside out, and he hasn't even touched—

"Ooooh," I moan on a breath when he dips his head between my legs, nuzzling my center with his nose.

"You smell so fucking good," he growls, the vibration from his words amplifying my pleasure.

With his focus below my waist, I make quick work of taking off my shirt and bra. After throwing them to the floor, I shove my fingers through his hair. I'm torn between holding him to me so I can enjoy the way his tongue teases my clit and pulling him away so I can have his cock instead.

I'm so close to coming, and I realize, almost too late, that I want him to come with me. So, I pull.

"Top nightstand drawer," I say, my tone breathless, before he can move up my body.

"Huh?"

"Condom."

Hurt flashes in his eyes, but he leans back and yanks the drawer open. After tearing open the foil packet with his teeth, he reaches between us to slide it over his hard shaft, but my hand stops him.

"You know this is my favorite part," I say, mimicking his earlier words.

I settle the rubber over his head and ease it down slowly. Ghost squeezes his eyes shut, and when the tips of my fingers touch his balls, he throws his head back.

"Not gonna last long, Em," he snarls, but there's no anger in his tone. "You know what this does to me."

I do. I remember what every one of my touches does to him. I remember it with stark clarity.

Deciding not to torture him, because let's face it, it's torture for me too, I line him up with my pussy. He doesn't hesitate as he thrusts… hard.

I cry out when he reaches the deepest part of me, the part that only he's ever been able to reach. Wrapping my legs around his hips, I dig my heels into his ass, doing my best to hold him as close as possible.

Ghost lifts himself up, bracing on his hands which are placed on either side of my head, and stares at me as he picks up his pace. I arch my back, silently begging him to pleasure me in other ways, and, like me, he remembers.

He latches onto a nipple, dragging it between his teeth, and the slight bit of stinging pain only ratchets up my desire.

"Fuck me," I plead. "Please fuck me harder."

There was a time that request freaked him out because, according to his younger self, he never wanted to hurt me. He has no such reservations now.

"Fuck you harder?" he grunts as he moves to the other nipple.

"Yes!" I shout. "God, yes!"

Abandoning my nipple, he slows his thrusts while he grabs my arms and stretches them above my head. He holds both wrists in one hand while the other he uses to hold himself upright. And then he moves faster, pistons in and out of me harder.

My hips buck, and I match his pace. I struggle against his hold, but I'm no match for his strength. No matter. Touching him with my hands would only lead to emotion entering the equation, and we can't have that.

With each thrust, he rolls his hips, giving me friction where I need it most.

"Come for me, Em," he demands roughly. "Come on my cock and drain me dry."

His harsh words are like a match lighting the tip of a fuse attached to a bomb. Fire sizzles from one nerve ending to the next, and I explode around his dick. Two more thrusts, and he detonates around me, swelling as he pumps me full.

After what feels like hours, our bodies still, and he rolls off to my side. I stare at the ceiling, my sanity returning, and can't help but wonder what the hell we just did.

"Bathroom?" he asks, taking the condom off.

I point to the door across the room that leads to the attached bath.

"Be right back."

He shuts the door behind him, and I take several deep breaths.

Fuck, fuck, fuck!

Scrambling off the bed, I yank open my bottom dresser drawer and grab the first pair of sleep shorts and tank that I find. By the time he returns from the bathroom, I'm dressed and sitting on the edge of the mattress, no doubt a stricken look on my face.

"What's this?" he asks, nodding at me.

"I… We…" Regret is a boulder in my chest, and I

have to clear my throat before I can force any more words out. "This doesn't change anything."

His expression falls, and his entire body tenses. A combination of pain and anger flashes across his face, and he busies himself with gathering his clothes and getting dressed.

"Parker?" I say, trying to get him to look at me.

"It's fucking Ghost," he barks, sliding his arms into his cut. He points to a patch affixed to the leather. "It even spells it out right here in case you ever forget."

Okay, so we're gonna do this the hard way.

"I'm sor—"

"Don't you dare say you're sorry," he seethes. "I can take a lot of shit from you, Em, but not that." He stalks to the bedroom door and pauses at the threshold, glancing over his shoulder. "Forget this ever happened. It was a mistake, clearly. Just…" He sighs. "I'll see you at my mom's, day after tomorrow."

And with that, he's gone, and I feel as though a bucket of ice has been poured over my body.

Crazy fucking day.

CHAPTER 11
GHOST

I forgot how to trust fifteen years ago.

"Parker, what are you doing here?"

I smile at my mom, who seems to have her wits about her today. Of course, it's still early, and mornings are always her best time.

"Thought I'd come for a visit," I tell her, as I sit at the kitchen table. "Whatcha cookin'?"

"I was hungry for an omelet, so I'm making one. I can make a second one if you're hungry."

"Sounds good to me," I say, a smile on my lips. It quickly fades when there's a knock on the door, and I'm reminded of why I'm really here. "Be right back."

I make my way through the living room, surprised Ember still showed up. After the other day,

I would've understood if she chose not to come. Fuck, I sorta hoped she wouldn't.

When I open the door, I swallow my tongue. Ember is wearing a pair of black scrubs with teal stethoscopes and heartbeats all over them. The outfit shouldn't be sexy, but on her, I fear even a paper bag would send all my blood straight to my cock.

"Can I come in or are you going to stare at me all day?" she asks sweetly.

I step aside and gesture for her to enter. As soon as she crosses the threshold, I close the door and turn around. Immediately, I recognize my mistake because she's taking in her surroundings, and all my eyes seem to see is her perfect ass.

Shaking my head, I clear my throat. "Where's your stuff?"

Ember whips around at the sound of my voice, slightly lifting the bag slung over her shoulder. I've got what I need for the day in here," she says. "The rest is in the car."

"Parker, your omelet's ready," Mom yells from the kitchen, preventing me from replying to Ember, and unlike when I speak, Ember's eyes light up, and a genuine smile graces her perfect lips.

Rolling my eyes, I ask, "Are you hungry?"

Ember shakes her head. "I grabbed a muffin on the way here. But I could go for some coffee."

"C'mon, then."

I move past her to head to the kitchen, and she follows. Mom is sitting at the table, already eating, and as soon as we enter the space, Mom's eyes widen, and she freezes with her fork halfway to her mouth.

After a moment's hesitation, she sets her fork down, and the light in her eyes dulls. "What's this?"

Pushing down my disappointment that her good day might have ended, I reply, "Mom, you remember Ember, right?"

"Hi Mrs. West," Ember greets. "It's been a long time."

Mom glares at her before shifting her attention to me. "What is she doing here?"

Shit. Her memory is still sharp as ever right now.

When I remain silent, Mom rises from her chair and stalks around the table to stand in front of Ember. "You break my son's heart, and you have the nerve to show your face here?" While it's a statement of fact—in her eyes at least—it comes out more like a question.

"Mom, ple—"

"It's okay," Ember says, not looking at me, her tone cheerier than the situation calls for. "Mrs. West, you're right. I hurt Parker, and for that, I'm so sorry."

Wait… What?

Mom's expression softens but barely. "Why are you here?"

"I'm here for you," Ember explains. "Parker thought that I could help you."

Mom's gaze whips to me. "What makes you think I need help?"

"I, um…" My throat goes dry, and words fail me.

"Mrs. West, why don't you finish your breakfast? I'm sure it'll taste better hot."

"Fine. But we're going to discuss this later," Mom huffs and returns to her food.

I practically drag Ember back into the living room while Mom is distracted.

"I'm so fucking sorry about that," I say, finding that I mean it. I shouldn't be because my mom was right about Ember breaking my heart, and she was only doing what mother's do. But Ember wouldn't be here if it weren't for me, and being attacked by the person she's here to help isn't what she signed on for.

"It's okay," she says. "I'm used to much worse, trust me."

Worse?

The thought of anyone treating her poorly boils my blood, and I mentally remind myself that I have no right to think that way. Not anymore.

"I'll talk to her, make her understand that you're not the enemy."

"No," she snaps. "I can handle this. I don't need you to fight my battles for me."

"I never said you did," I say, my teeth clenched. "Ya know what? Never mind. It doesn't seem to matter what I fucking do or say, it's the wrong thing with you."

Ember's stiff shoulders drop, the fight leaving her. "I'm here for your mom, not us. Can't we just keep things professional?"

"Professional? How are we sup—"

My phone rings, cutting me off, and I curse under my breath. I pull it out of my back pocket, and a quick glance at the screen tells me it's not a call I can ignore.

"I gotta take this," I tell her before answering. "Hey, Crow, what's up?"

Moving to the hallway so I can have a little privacy, I have a half-hearted conversation with my president about how things are going here, all the while, Ember's eyes are on me.

"Yeah, yeah, things are okay," I tell him. "I'll be there within the hour."

"Are you sure?" he asks. "Poker can handle this alone."

"I'm sure. Honestly, I could use some time in the Nightmare Room."

He chuckles. "I'm sure you could. See ya when

you get here."

"Right. Later, brother."

As I disconnect the call, my feet eat up the space between me and the woman from my past.

"Everything okay?" she asks, seemingly genuinely concerned.

"Yep."

She eyes me warily. "Are yo—"

"Parker, sweetheart, your breakfast is getting cold," Mom says as she makes her way into the living room. Her face lights up when she sees Ember. "Oh, hi, honey," she greets. "Parker didn't tell me you were coming. But I'm so glad you did because we've got a lot of last-minute details to work out."

Confusion wrinkles my brow, but Ember only smiles. "Hi, Mrs. West."

Mom waves her hand dismissively. "Pft. How many times do I have to tell you to call me 'Mom'?"

Well, fuck.

Ember glances at me, pity in her blue eyes. I hate that look. Anger, rage, even hatred I can deal with, but pity? Nope.

"Yes, ma'am. Why don't you come sit down while I finish talking to Parker, and then we can work on those details later?"

"Sit down?" Mom shakes her head. "Oh, no. There's no time to waste. The wedding is in…" She settles her hands on her hips. "Well, I don't quite recall when it is, but it's soon, right?"

"We've got time, Mrs. West."

Mom glances at me, and I force myself to nod, to reassure her that there's plenty of time.

"If you say so," Mom mutters as she moves to the couch and sits.

Ember levels her gaze on mine and nods to the kitchen. I follow her there, my stomach churning at how quickly the morning shifted.

"It's going to be okay," she tells me.

"She's in there convinced that we're still together, on the verge of getting married, and you expect me to believe that shit is okay?"

"This is my job," she insists. "If you want me to work here, I'm gonna need you to trust me."

Trust? She talks of trust after all we've been through? I forgot how to trust fifteen years ago.

"Yeah, okay," I acquiesce. "I've gotta go take care of some things. Will you be okay with her?"

Ember smirks. "I repeat, this is my job. We'll be fine."

"Right."

"Look, Parker, I'll call you if I need to, but otherwise, let me do my thing, okay?"

"Ghost," I correct out of habit.

"Ghost," she repeats.

"I'll be back later to check in," I tell her.

She shrugs. "Okay, if you think that's necessary."

I huff out a humorless laugh. "I have no intention of simply dumping her on you. I'm not sure what kind of families you're used to dealing with, but I didn't hire you because I don't give two shits about her. I hired you because I love her, and I'm not stupid enough to think I can give her everything she needs."

"Never thought otherwise."

I stare at her as if I'll find a lie in her expression, but all I see is sincerity. First pity, now this? I can't fucking handle it.

"I gotta go," I say, pushing past her. "Call me if you need anything."

I kiss my mom on the top of her head as I walk past toward the door. Before I can close it behind me, I hear my mom ask Ember who the nice man who just left was.

Mom thinks Ember broke my heart, and she's not wrong. But now she's breaking it all over again.

CHAPTER 12
EMBER

I'm an employee, nothing more, nothing less.

"How are you, really?"

Tears threaten to spill over my lashes at the concern in Lori's voice. We've been best friends for as long as I can remember, and she's the only person in my life who knows how long it took to piece myself back together after breaking off my engagement to Ghost.

"I'm fine." My voice cracks, giving away the lie.

"Bullshit. I know you, Em. Sometimes more than you know yourself, I'm afraid."

Sighing, I swipe at the wetness on my cheeks. "Why did I agree to do this?"

My first day with Mrs. West—I can't bring myself to call her 'Mom' no matter how many times she insists—has been torture. One minute, I'm the enemy, and the next, I'm her future daughter-in-law. I should've expected it, but I failed to realize how hard it would be to work with a patient who I've got a history with.

"There's a reason doctors aren't supposed to treat family members," Lori says, echoing my thoughts.

"She's not family," I insist.

"Close enough."

"How am I going to get through this, Lor?" I ask. "It could be years before the disease takes her. Years!"

"You can always tell Parker th—"

"Ghost," I correct her, hating myself for it.

"What?"

I heave a sigh and lie back on the bed in my temporary bedroom. "It's Ghost now."

"Oh, yeah." She laughs. "I forgot he's a big bad biker."

It's on the tip of my tongue to defend him, but I don't. Why should I? "Anyway, you were saying?"

"Tell *Ghost* that you can't do it," she finishes her earlier thought. "Recommend another nurse for him and bail."

I'd be lying if I said the thought hadn't crossed my mind. It definitely has… dozens of times.

"I can't."

"Why not?"

"Because. I just… can't."

"More like you won't."

"That too."

"But why? I don't understand why you're punishing yourself like this."

"I'm not punishing myself."

"Yeah, you are," she snaps. "Just like you did after he moved to Oregon."

"This has nothing to do with that."

"Doesn't it?" she counters. "Admit it, if this were any other patient, you'd have been out the door by now."

She's wrong about that, but it's not surprising. Lori never did understand how I could work with people whose disease causes them to treat me like shit half the time.

"I've never walked out on a job, and I'm not gonna start now."

There's a long pause as if she's biting back some retort that will piss me off. "Okay," she finally says. "What can I do to make this better? How can I help?"

"I don't know," I answer honestly. "I just have to treat this like any other job, right?"

"Right," she agrees, her tone too bright, too agreeable. "What if we have a girl's night soon? When will you get time off?"

"I've got one day a week off," I tell her. "And before you tell me that's insane, it was my idea."

"Wasn't gonna say any such thing," she quips.

I laugh. "Uh huh."

"Okay, fine, I was. But I won't now."

"Thanks, Lor."

"You're welcome. So, when is your day off?"

"Um, I don't know. I didn't get a chance to talk to Ghost about it before he had to go this morning. He said he'd be back, but…" I pull the phone away from my ear and glance at the time, and annoyance flares when I see that it's after ten. "Well, it's late, so I guess it'll have to wait until tomorrow."

Or whenever he decides to show his face again.

"As soon as you do know, call me. We'll figure something out."

"I will," I promise her.

"Okay. Try to have a good night."

"You, too. Love ya."

"Back at ya."

I disconnect the call before getting to my feet to go check on Mrs. West. She went to bed an hour ago, after I assured her that I'd make myself at home. I wasn't the enemy an hour ago.

The woman is sleeping soundly, and I leave her bedroom door cracked so I can hear her if she gets up in the middle of the night. I learned the hard way with my very first patient that sometimes, they wake and get confused which can lead to a walk to nowhere in particular.

Just as I'm about to shut off the last light in the living room, a sound at the front door pulls my focus from my task. A second later, Ghost walks in like he owns the place.

Well, it is his mother's house, the house he grew up in.

"What are you doing here?" I hiss, my voice barely above a whisper.

"Hi to you too," he says dryly.

"Do you have any idea what time it is?" I demand.

"Do you have any idea whose house you're in?" he counters, and I press my lips together. "That's better. Now, I'm sorry it's late, but this was the earliest I could get here. I told you I'd be back, and I didn't want to make a liar out of myself."

Oh, well… That's kinda sweet.

"Oh."

He smirks, and my stomach flips over on itself. Dammit, that smirk always could knock the wind out of my sails.

"How was today? Wanting to run screaming for the hills yet?"

"No, I'm not gonna run. As for today, it was… good."

He takes a step toward me. "Ember Tamlin, are you lying to me?"

"No. It was good. We had our bumps, but your mom is safe and sound in bed."

"I was more worried about you."

"I thought you said you didn't want to be a liar."

He huffs out a laugh. "Seriously, how was she today?"

"She was fine. Good moments and bad, but that's normal."

We spend the next half hour discussing his mother and all the ways in which he's seen her slipping away from him. Several times I find myself having to hold back the comfort I want to offer. That's not my place anymore. I'm an employee, nothing more, nothing less.

And a one-time only one-night stand.

By the time he leaves, a promise to relieve me for a day off in three days, my nerves are fried.

You can do this, Ember. You have to do this.

CHAPTER 13
GHOST

I was her first, and I should've been her last, her only.

Two weeks later…

"Figured I'd find you here."

I lift my beer to my lips and down what remains in the bottle before signaling to the bartender for another. It doesn't surprise me that Poker tracked me down. Ballinger's is the only place a brother goes when he wants to drink but not party. And I definitely don't feel like a fucking party.

"Here I am," I confirm.

"What can I get ya?" Meri, the bartender, asks him as she sets a fresh bottle in front of me.

"I'll have what he's having," Poker replies. "And two shots of Jack."

"Comin' right up."

"Why aren't you at the clubhouse?" I ask. "Figured you'd be all over Kitty tonight."

"She was hooking up with Screamer when I left," he says, annoyance coloring the words. "Bitch is about to find out how good she has it with me."

I chuckle. "Keep talking about her like that, and it's no wonder she's fucking him instead of you."

"You're one to talk," he snaps, but there's no heat in his tone. "You haven't fucked a club whore in, what? Weeks?"

I don't bother correcting him. It's been much longer than weeks. I push that depressing thought away because it also serves as a reminder that it's been two weeks since I was inside Ember, and thinking about that hardens my cock to a painful degree.

"Do you really think Limitless Throttle has nothing to do with the wave of drugs hitting the streets?" I ask, desperate to change the subject.

He shrugs. "Crow seems to believe it, and that's good enough for me."

"Yeah, I guess. But who the fuck else could it be?"

Poker snorts. "Seriously? How about anyone with a grudge against the club? Not exactly a small list."

"No, definitely not fucking small. But we've taken out five low level dealers, and none of them talked," I remind him. "The Nightmare Room is meant to provoke death-bed-like confessions, and it's not. *We're* not. What could possibly be scarier than a Soulless King torturing you in that space?"

He rests his elbows on the bar, thoughtfully staring at nothing. "We're missing something."

"No shit. But what?"

"If I knew, we wouldn't be having this conversation," he gripes.

"True."

"Enough about that crap. How's your mom doing? The new nurse is working out?"

I turn to face him, stare at him for a moment to determine if he knows more than I've told him. There's nothing in his gaze but genuine curiosity.

"Mom's okay. She seems to like the nurse, thank fuck."

And that's the truth. Sure, they have their moments where Mom recognizes her as the girl from my past, but mostly she only remembers tidbits from before our breakup. I don't know which is worse… Mom planning a wedding that will never happen or her hating Ember.

"That's good," Poker states. "Hey, maybe you could introduce me to this nurse of hers." He bobs his eyebrows. "As long as Kitty's otherwise engaged, I wouldn't mind a little tender love and care from someone else."

My hackles rise, and I grab him by his cut, hauling him off the stool. "You fucking touch her, and I'll kill you," I snarl.

Poker's eyes widen with shock, and he holds his hands up. "Whoa, brother, chill the fuck out."

"Ember is off-limits, got it?"

"Ember, huh?" He grins. "I bet she's fire in the sack."

I lean forward and practically hit his nose with mine. "Are you really this stupid?" I growl, rage burning me from the inside out.

Logically, I know I'm overreacting. I have no claim on Ember and certainly no right to act like this when that's the case. But the thought of another man, a *brother*, touching her makes me want to burn the world to the ground.

"Get it? Ember... fire?" he snickers.

I shove him away, and if it weren't for his quick reflexes, he'd be on his ass. "Jesus, I'm just kidding. What is wrong with you?"

"Nothing's wrong with me," I snap. "But she's off-limits."

"Yeah, I get it. But why?" He holds my stare, and I know the moment realization dawns because his brows shoot up. "Oh, it's like that, is it?"

"It's not like anything."

"And I'm Mother Teresa," he deadpans.

That statement does the trick and snaps me out of my fury. I return to my stool and lift my beer. It's warm now, but I don't care.

"So, what's up?" he prods. "This Ember chick mean something to you?"

A grunt is my only response.

"Okay, fine. Don't tell me. But get your shit together or I won't be the only one asking questions."

He downs the remainder of his drink and both forgotten shots before tossing a twenty on the bar and heading for the door. Now that I'm alone again, I let my mind wander.

He's right, of course. I do need to get my shit together. If for no other reason than I have no business feeling possessive of a woman who doesn't want me. She didn't back then, and she doesn't now.

The problem is, I don't know how to feel about that. I thought I was over her. Hell, she and I both moved on with our lives as soon as I moved away from Marble Falls. I wasn't celibate that whole time, and I'm sure she wasn't either.

At the thought, my fists clench. I was her first, and I should've been her last, her only. But life had other plans… She had other plans.

"Gimme another beer," I demand when Meri steps in front of me. She narrows her eyes, and I force a smile. "Please."

"That's better," she says. "Geez, just because you're a badass doesn't mean you get to be an asshole."

Is she flirting? I feel like she's flirting.

"You're right," I say, uncomfortable with my line of thought. "Sorry."

"No problem."

I spend the rest of the night getting drunk and arguing with myself about women and whether or not I need them in my life, whether or not there's a certain one that I want in my life.

When Meri announces last call, I'm beyond any ability to get myself home, let alone stand up.

"I'm gonna call one of your brothers to come get you," she says.

"I'm 'kay," I slur. "I can 'rive."

She laughs at me. "No, you can't. Hand over your keys."

"No."

Without missing a beat, she walks around the bar and reaches into my pocket to grab said keys. "You're so damn toasted, you didn't even try to fight me off."

"So?"

"So, I'm calling someone to come get you. If there's someone you'd rather I make that call to than one of your brothers, I suggest you tell me now."

She reaches into my pocket again and grabs my cell. I try to get to my feet, and my head swims.

"Fuck," I mumble.

"Yeah, fuck," she mocks. I watch helplessly as she scrolls through my contacts.

Her gaze shifts to mine for a second before she grins wickedly and taps the screen and holds the cell to her ear. I have no idea what her grin means, but I find out the moment she opens her mouth. "Hi, is this Ember?"

Double fuck.

CHAPTER 14
EMBER

AND YOU CARE BECAUSE?

"Hi, is this Ember?"

It's two in the morning and this bitch doesn't know for sure who she's calling? And why is she calling from Ghost's phone? I roll over and rest my arm over my eyes, blocking out the light from the hallway that I always leave on for Mrs. West.

"Who's this?" I ask.

"My name is Meri, and I'm here at Ballinger's with Ghost."

My entire body tenses at her words. It makes sense, since it was his name that popped up on my screen, but still. Is this some sort of joke? "Good for you."

"Oh, no," she says with a laugh. "It's not like that. I'm the bartender here, and he's drunk as shit."

"And you called me because?"

"Well, because he needs a ride home, and he didn't want me to call one of his brothers."

"Did he ask you to call me?"

"No, but he—"

"He won't like that you called me."

Do I like that she did?

"Based on the glare I'm getting at the moment, I gathered as much." She pauses, mumbles something to Ghost, no doubt, before continuing. "Look, I can drive him home when I'm done here, but the clubhouse is a half hour in the wrong direction."

I sigh. Ghost and I have managed to avoid each other since the day I started working for me… mostly. Everything has remained very brief and professional. He comes to give me my day off, and the second he shows up, I'm out the door. The same thing happens when I return, but in reverse. It's like he can't stand to be around me.

I should be grateful, happy that he's not reading more into this whole situation than is there, but I find that all I am is… sad.

"You said you're at Ballinger's?" I finally ask.

"Yep."

Sighing, I throw the covers to the side and get out of bed. "Give me twenty, and I'll be there."

"Thanks, bye."

Meri disconnects the call as if she's afraid I'll change my mind. Hell, I probably will… over and over again until I have no choice but to follow through because he'll be right in front of me.

Before I get dressed, I send a text to one of the emergency numbers Ghost left for me in case I couldn't get a hold of him.

> Me: I'm so sorry to bother you, but I just got a call from the bartender at Ballinger's. Ghost told me to call/text if I ever needed anything. I'm afraid to leave his mother alone while I go get him. Any chance you could pick him up?

I stare at my phone as three bouncing dots quickly appear, signaling a response.

> Crow: Hi Ember. You can always call/text if you need something. Day or night. I can't go get him though bc I'm tied up with club business. I'm sure his mom will be fine.

> Me: Not sure I should take that chance.

> Crow: Can you take her with you?

> Me: It's 2 in the morning!

> Crow: I know. Look, I'll send a prospect to sit on the house while you're gone.

> Me: Can't the prospect pick him up?

Why is he making this so hard?

> Crow: We don't have a vehicle available at the moment for that and based on the fact that he needs a ride, I'm guessing he won't last on the back of a bike

> Me: Fine. How fast can the prospect get here?

I start to get dressed as I wait for his reply. It takes a bit longer than the others, which fuels my annoyance. After several minutes, my phone dings.

> Crow: Ben should be there in 10. Mrs. West will be okay by herself for a few. Go ahead and leave.

Grudgingly, I type out one last text.

> Me: Thanks

It takes me a few more minutes to gather my

purse and grab a bottle of water. Dumbass is probably gonna need something to drink that's not booze.

And you care because?

Unease settles in my gut as I drive down the street, away from the house, but the rumble of a motorcycle reaches my ears when I turn to head further into town. Good, Ben must be close. At least I can worry a little less about Mrs. West.

Now I can focus all my worry on myself and the stupid man I'm playing designated driver for.

CHAPTER 15
GHOST

Parker died when you left him.

"Your ride's here."

I lift my head off the bar and smile at Meri. Being mad at her took too much effort, so I decided to let it go. Besides, Ember's picking me up, and that can only mean good things… right?

I'm sure if I were sober, I'd be thinking much differently.

"'Kay."

When I try to stand, all I manage is to slide off the stool and land on my ass. I'm sure I'd feel pain, but the alcohol is dulling all my senses.

"I shoulda left you here," Ember sasses when she gets to me and stands at my side.

"Aw, c'mon," I whine.

"Don't," she snaps. "I had to leave your mom alone to come pick your drunk ass up."

I screw up my face, trying like hell to remember why she'd be with my mom, but for the life of me, I can't.

"She'll be 'kay."

"Dammit, Ghost," Ember huffs.

"Um, I don't mean to interrupt," Meri says. "But I really need to get home. I've got class in the morning, and I'm beat. Let me help you get him out to the car, and the two of you can fight there."

The two women manage to get me to my feet, which is no small feat considering I tower over both of them. Each wraps an arm around my back, and heat courses through me, but only on my right side, the side Ember is on.

Huh.

When we step outside, the cool night air does little to sober me up. I stumble along with them as we traipse toward Ember's car, which she parked a few spaces down from the bar. I almost lose my balance a few times, but they keep me upright.

After they get me settled into the passenger seat, Ember slams the door. I watch as she talks to Meri for a few minutes before sliding into the driver's seat and glaring at me.

"Put your seatbelt on," she orders.

"Yes, ma'am."

My hands don't cooperate, and after the third failed attempt, Ember grumbles and buckles me in herself. Then she thrusts a bottle of water at me.

"Drink this, and for the love of all that's holy, don't puke in my car."

"Like it when you're bossy."

I don't miss the small smile she tries so hard to squash. "Shut up."

Twice, she has to pull over so I can vomit without ruining her precious car, and both times, she seems more worried than angry. I haven't been this drunk in a long time, but I'm not so far gone that she should worry.

But I can't say it doesn't feel a little nice that she does.

"Home sweet home," she chirps after parking her car in the driveway.

I look at the house and narrow my eyes. Ben is sitting on the top porch step looking like he hasn't a care in the world.

"What's wrong?" Ember asks, noticing the way I tense at the sight of him.

"What the fuck's he doin' here?"

"I couldn't very well leave your mom alone, could I?"

Instantly, I relax, although it's not hard to do considering my condition. "Oh, right."

"If I didn't know any better, I'd say you're jealous, Parker West."

Rather than respond, I climb out of the car, sending up a silent thanks to whatever God is out there that I don't fall over again.

"You can go," I say when I reach Ben.

"Okay." He shrugs and hops off the steps. "Have a good night." As he passes Ember, he says, "If you need anything else, call, okay?"

"I will, thanks."

"No problem."

Ember closes the distance between us and glares at me. "Stop acting like a dog pissing on his territory," she snaps. "You're my employer, that's it."

The alcohol clouding my judgment is not my friend at the moment. Hell, I don't know that it ever was, yet here I am.

Without thinking, I reach for her and pull her lips to mine. She tastes like mint, and I revel in it. For a moment, she capitulates and kisses me back, but only for a moment. Then she seems to come to some sort of decision and pushes me away.

"No, Parker. We can't do this."

"Why not?" I counter. "We're both adults, and it doesn't have to mean anything."

I swear pain flashes in her blue eyes, but she quickly masks it and squares her shoulder. "That's exactly why. Because it won't mean anything, and I'm not that kinda girl."

"Coulda fooled me."

The second the words are out of my mouth, I want to call them back. Even hammered, I know they're wrong. And Ember doesn't let me off the hook easily. Her palm connects with my cheek, and the sting chases away the booze more than anything else could have.

"You're a dick, Parker, ya know that?"

She doesn't give me a chance to answer before stomping onto the porch and unlocking the front door, but my voice stops her in her tracks.

"It's. Ghost. Parker died when you left him."

CHAPTER 16
EMBER

You! You were more important. You've always been more fucking important!

"What can I do to make it better?"

I stare at Lori, her face a blur through my tears. It's been a week since I broke things off with Parker, and I've done nothing but cry. Lori has been with me every free moment she has, but I can't expect her to keep it up. I have to find a way to pull myself together.

"I th-thought he'd fi-fight for me," I cry.

She wraps her arm around me. "I know, hon. Honestly, I did, too."

"Why d-didn't he?"

"I don't know. Maybe you should call him, talk to him about it," she suggests, not for the first time. "You guys

have been together since middle school. Surely, he doesn't want this to end either."

I wipe my nose on the sleeve of my hoodie. "I can't c-call him."

"Why not?"

Why not, indeed?

Shuddering, I hiccup several times as I try to pull myself together. "Because, if he wanted to be with me, he'd pick up the damn phone."

She snorts. "Parker's a guy. Guys are stupid."

"You said it yourself, we'd been together since middle school. He knows he can call me."

"Does he, Em? Because from what you've told me, you made it pretty clear that you were done."

As my best friend, it's her prerogative to call me out on my bullshit, but it doesn't mean I've gotta like it. Signing, I decide that maybe she's right. Maybe I should call him.

"Fine. Hand me the phone," *I grumble, pointing to the cordless sitting on the arm of the couch in my apartment.*

Lori grins like a kid on Christmas, her hope flaring, and it's impossible not to feel a little myself. But as soon as I make the call, any hope is immediately snatched away.

"Ember, honestly, why are you calling?" Mrs. West says once I identify myself.

"I just want to talk to Parker," I say. "Please."

"Even if I wanted to let you talk to him, you can't."

"But… why?" I work hard to keep my lower lip from wobbling.

"He's gone, Ember. Left for Oregon two days ago. Said there was no point in waiting since you aren't getting married and that staying here to possibly run into you in town would be worse than death."

My heart cracks wider than I thought possible. "Oh."

"Now, if there's nothing else, I've got to finish dinner before Mr. West gets home."

"Right, um, no, there's nothing else. Thank you."

"Goodbye, Ember."

She hangs up before I can say anything else.

I bolt upright in bed, my shorts and tank top sticking to my clammy skin. I haven't had that dream in years, the one that reminds me very acutely of how big of a fool I was when I was younger.

No, I wasn't a fool. I did what I had to do.

Still telling yourself that, hmm?

Sunshine peeks through the curtains, and a quick glance at my cell tells me I overslept. Probably because I had to make a middle of the night trip, but oh well. It is what it is.

I take a quick shower and dress for the day before heading to the kitchen where I hear Mrs. West humming.

"Morning," I say brightly. "How'd you sleep?"

"Much better than Parker, that's for sure," she

says, her tone cheerful. "Poor thing must've had too much to drink because he's passed out on the porch."

"What?" I screech, hurrying to the front door.

I yank it open and freeze when I see him curled up on the welcome mat like a dog trying to sleep in a bed too small for them. Gently, I nudge him with my bare foot in an effort to wake him up.

"Five more minutes," he mumbles, his Texan accent stronger than I've heard it since seeing him again.

"No," I say, speaking loud enough to break through his hangover. "Get up."

As if I poked him with a branding iron, he sits up, then holds his hands to his head with a scowl. "Dammit, that hurt."

"I'm sure it did. Now get up and get inside before the neighbors see you out here like a homeless person."

I spin on my heel and walk away, not bothering to wait and see if he follows. It's not my house, after all, and I'm not his mother. Speaking of, I don't hear her humming anymore, and the house is eerily silent.

Shit!

"Mrs. West," I call out. No response. "Mrs. West," I try again as I race through the living room to the kitchen, finding it empty. The stove, however, is on and a pot is boiling over.

"Why are you yelling?" Ghost asks from behind me. "Use your inside voice."

"I'm yelling because while I was dealing with you, your mom disappeared," I reply frantically and rush down the hall to check the bedrooms and bathrooms.

"What do you mean she disappeared?" he snarls, all traces of his rough night gone. "You're supposed to be watching her."

"No shit, asshole! But she said you were sleeping on the porch, and I—" I clamp my mouth shut before I say something I can't take back.

"You what?" he demands. "What could possibly have been more important than your damn job?"

His taunt causes my vision to go red. Rage bubbles up the back of my throat, and I can't stop myself from shouting my reply.

"You! You were more important. You've always been more fucking important!"

CHAPTER 17
GHOST

EM'S A FUCKIN' ANGEL.

"SHE CAN'T BE FAR."

I force a smile I don't feel when I glance at Ember. Ever since her very loud declaration, we've been focusing on finding my mom. She's never walked off like this before, and with every passing minute, the dread in my gut intensifies. Since it's been two hours of fruitless searching, the intensity is close to unbearable.

"I think I should call the cops," I say, going against everything I've learned since becoming a Soulless King. "It's been too long."

"Call the club," she counters. "And Addison. They'll be able to help more than the police."

"Addison is police," I remind her.

"She's also family." Ember finally levels her gaze on mine. "I get the urge to call the cops, I really do. But I've dealt with this, and calling them could trigger an investigation with Adult Protective Services. You don't want that, trust me."

I stiffen at the implication of her words. "They'd be stupid as fuck to accuse me of anything bad."

"Yeah, they would, but that wouldn't stop them. And if Addison comes as a cop, she'll be bound by the rules. If she comes as family…" She shrugs. "It's different."

I'm surprised she's suggesting I don't involve law enforcement, and I'm even more surprised that I thought it would be a good idea. I'm a former undercover cop who quit because of the shit dirty cops pulled… the last thing I need is one of them in my business or trying too hard to please an even dirtier higher up.

"Thanks," I say as I pull my cell out of my cut to call Crow.

"For what?" she asks while I wait for him to answer.

"For understanding what my emotions wouldn't let me remember."

"That sounds serious," Crow says, pulling my attention away from Ember.

"Hey, Pres, I've got a problem."

"What's that?"

"Mom took off about two hours ago, and we can't find her. I know you're working on some other things, but any chance you can spare some of the guys? We could use all the help we can get." I pause. "Oh, and is Addison off today? I'd like her help, too, but not in an official capacity if you get my drift."

"We'll all be there in ten. Send me your current location."

"Crow, you don't ha—"

"We'll *all* be there," he snarls. "Family is more important than anything else, whether by blood or the patch, got me?"

"Got you."

"Good. Send Tracer your mom's cell number. Maybe he can track her that way. Honestly, for a former cop, I'm surprised you didn't think to call sooner. And as a brother, I'm a little pissed that you didn't."

"Yeah, well, took me a bit to think of it," I say, sliding my eyes to Ember.

"You mean it took a pretty woman to get you to think clearly," he teases.

I chuckle. "Something like that."

"Send that info. See ya soon."

He disconnects the call, and I send off two quick texts before tucking my cell back into my cut.

"They're on their way," I tell Ember as I walk to where she's standing down the block. She walked away to give me privacy, and I'm grateful for it.

"Told ya."

"Yeah, you did." I rock on my heels. "Now what?"

God, I *am* an idiot. I used to search for people for a living—sort of—and now I'm relying on a nurse to tell me what to do.

"We keep searching."

"Really, I don't know what all the fuss is about."

I grind my molars together to keep from yelling at my mom. It took two more hours, ten Soulless Kings other than me, Addison, and Ember to track her to the train station on the other end of town. Tracer would've found her sooner, no doubt, but she forgot to charge her phone overnight, and it was deader than a doornail.

"We were worried about you, Mrs. West," Crow

says, slipping his arm through hers to lead her to Ember's car, which Addison took her back to the house to retrieve when Mom refused to get in anyone else's vehicle.

"Oh, pish posh," she says, smacking Crow on his forearm. "Trace Thompson, I've known you since you were a little boy. It's my job to worry, not yours."

He smiles. "Yes, ma'am."

When I asked her why she'd been at the train station, she scolded me for not remembering that my father was returning from a business trip. She was simply going to meet him so she'd be the first thing he saw when he stepped foot in Marble Falls again.

I didn't have the heart to remind her that Dad's dead, and apparently, neither did anyone else because no one said a damn thing. Eventually, her memory shifted, and she was in the present. It took a little bit of explaining for her to understand how she got to the train station, but she seems no worse for the wear, so we've all let it go.

"Parker, sweetheart," Mom says, looking over her shoulder at me. "You'll ride with Ember and me back to the house, right?"

"Yeah, Mom, I will."

Crow hands her off to Addison, who gets her settled into the passenger seat.

"I'm glad she's okay," Crow says to me, his voice low. "What about you?"

"I'm glad too."

"No, I meant, are you okay? I know this scared the shit out of you."

I thrust a hand through my hair and sigh. "I'm fine. Just glad this turned out the way it did. Could've been a lot worse."

"Yeah, it could've been, but it wasn't. Focus on that, yeah?"

"I'm tryin', Pres, but it's fucking hard."

"No doubt it's harder with the situation with Ember?"

I stiffen. "What situation?"

"Calm your tits, man," he cajoles. "I just meant that it has to be hard being around her again."

"Oh, right. It's not easy, I'll give ya that. But…"

"But what?" he prods when I fall silent.

I glance at Ember, who's chatting happily with my mother while they wait on me. "Look at 'em. She's the best person for my mom. She handles everything Mom throws at her with grace and a smile. Em's a fuckin' angel."

"Jesus, you're getting poetic."

"What?" I narrow my eyes at him. "No, I'm not. Just stating facts."

"Right. Keep telling yourself that." He pauses to

kiss Addison's cheek when she joins us. "So, if she's treating your mom with grace and a smile, how's she treating you?" he asks me.

I scowl. "With attitude and more fuckin' attitude."

CHAPTER 18
EMBER

I really need to have a conversation with him about the last fifteen years.

"I'm surprised Parker hasn't returned."

I swallow the bite of spaghetti in my mouth and nod at Mrs. West. It's been two days since her *adventure*, as we've been calling it, and Ghost has yet to show his face again at the house. I don't know if he's mad at me for what happened or if something else is going on, but I'm a little worried. He's invested in his mother's care, whether I'm here or not, and to not show up after the other day is odd.

"I'm sure he'll come by soon," I assure her, even though I have no clue if I'm right. "He's probably busy with stuff at the club."

"Mmm," she hums, taking another bite of her

dinner. "That little club of his has been so good for him."

I refrain from telling her that that 'little club' is a one percenter biker club that requires her son to do all manner of things. What things, you ask… Well, I don't know exactly. He and I haven't talked about it. We haven't talked about anything deeper than what lies on the surface.

Maybe you should.

In a town as small as Marble Falls, I was shocked to learn that Ghost had returned, and I knew nothing about it. I guess I did a better job than I realized at blocking out all the gossip. Either that or the fact that he went by Ghost instead of Parker had something to do with my ignorance of the facts. As far as I'd been concerned, he'd still been in Oregon, likely married with kids and a dog.

Never in a million years would I have thought he'd be back here, no longer in law enforcement, and I certainly wouldn't have guessed I'd be working for him.

I really need to have a conversation with him about the last fifteen years.

As soon as the thought enters my mind, it dawns on me how much I actually *want* to have that conversation. Not because I want to rehash the past or our failed relationship, but because I genuinely want to know about him, the man he is now.

"Did you hear that?" Mrs. West asks, pulling me out of my head.

Stilling, I listen, fully expecting there to be no sound, but then I hear it. A knock on the door.

I smile at her. "Expecting anyone?" She shakes her head. "Okay, be right back."

It couldn't be Ghost because he wouldn't bother knocking. I suppose it could be Lori. She knows where to find me, and after ensuring it would be okay with Ghost and his mom, I told her to stop by any time, but she'd call or text first.

The knocking stops by the time I reach the front door, and when I open it, the porch is empty. I step outside and glance up and down the street but don't see anyone or any vehicles that shouldn't be there. Unease washes over me, and when I turn around to go back inside and spot the piece of paper affixed to the door, that unease swells into a tidal wave.

What the hell?

I yank the paper off the door and carry it inside, locking the door behind me.

"Who is it?" Mrs. West calls from the kitchen. "I hope you invited them in."

"It was no one," I reply, forcing my tone to remain neutral. "They had the wrong house."

"Oh, pity. I do love company."

"I'm gonna run to the bathroom real quick. Are you okay in there?"

"I'm fine, Ember. You and my son worry too much."

With good reason.

I walk to the bathroom, paper in hand, so she doesn't get suspicious. Only once I'm there do I unfold the note and scan its contents. The handwriting is messy, almost illegible, but I manage to make them out enough that my stomach bottoms out.

He thinks he can protect you. He thinks you're untouchable because you're not a club member. He's wrong. There is nothing the Soulless Kings can do to keep you safe, nothing the former piggy can do to stop me from raining down all sorts of hell. Tell him and the others to back the fuck off before they force my hand. I don't like to hurt people who don't ask for it, but I will. And I'll do it with a smile on my face.

The note isn't signed, and it's not clear if it's meant for Mrs. West or me. Not that it matters. Whoever wrote it, whoever it's designed to scare, the message is clear: tell Ghost and the club to stop whatever it is they're doing or else.

I flush the toilet to keep up the illusion that I'm really going to the bathroom, and then I make my way back to the kitchen, shoving the note in the pocket of my jeans as I go. I need to call Ghost and tell him about this, but I'll finish dinner first, so I don't have to explain anything to Mrs. West. No reason to scare her, too.

We finish our spaghetti and then work together to get our mess cleaned up. As soon as that's taken care of, I get her settled in the living room to watch Jeopardy and head to my room to make that phone call.

"You've reached Ghost," his voicemail greets me. "I can't come to the phone for one reason or another—"

Practically growling, I disconnect the call. Why isn't he answering? He always answers because he knows I only call when it concerns his mom. I try three more times, hoping like hell that he just didn't get to his cell in time, but I get the same result: no answer. Switching to text, I type out a quick message, one designed to scare him as much as the note is scaring me.

> Me: Got a major poblem… CALL ME NOW!

CHAPTER 19
GHOST

We'll finally get to live together like we were supposed to.

"Who the fuck do you work for?"

Poker and I have been in the Nightmare Room with Monty, the latest dealer slinging Soulless Kings shit laced with Fentanyl, for three hours. The guy's clinging to life, his breathing shallow and his heartbeat slow as molasses. He's close to giving up his employer, so fucking close. Hell, he's almost spilled the beans a few times already.

Monty tries to shake his head, and whimpers in pain at the movement. "He'll kill me."

"He won't get the chance," I snarl, holding the lit torch to the bottom of his feet. It's easy to do with him dangling from chains attached to the ceiling.

Monty screams, and the concrete space swallows up the sound. There's not a soul on the planet other than Poker and me who can hear him now.

Poker reaches into his pocket and pulls out the baggie we confiscated from Monty when we brought him here. The little pills are marked with the Soulless King brand, but they're a light green when ours are white. And we don't aim to kill anyone. These little green tablets are designed with that specific purpose in mind.

"Give us a name, and we can make this a little less painful for you," my brother says, holding the baggie in front of Monty's face and shrugging. "Yeah, you'll still die, but you'll go out on a high."

A total of forty-three people have died since some jackass put these pills on the streets, forty-three people who might not lead the best life or make the best choices. That doesn't mean they deserved to die, especially when their addiction is punishment enough for their decisions.

Of those forty-three, eleven have been minors. Soulless Kings aren't saints by any means, but our dealers know better than to sell to kids. Doing so is a one-way ticket to meet their maker.

When Monty says nothing, I glance at Poker. "Bro, he's not gonna give it up. Let's end this and move on."

Poker hesitates, as I knew he would, and stares at Monty. He's giving the guy a chance to change his mind, a few moments to let the fear of a painful death override his fear of his boss. Like Poker said, we're still gonna end his miserable life, of that he has no choice, but he can choose how it happens… kinda.

"Okay," Poker finally says as he moves to the wall and grabs the scythe from its perch. "I'll gut him, and you shove the torch up his ass."

Monty's eyes widen as far as the swelling allows, which admittedly isn't much, and he thrashes against the chains. "No. No, wait. Just… w-wait."

"We're done waiting," I snarl, walking around to his back.

"I-I'll talk, okay?" he cries. "I'll g-give you what y-you want."

I turn the torch off and return to his front. "You've got two seconds or—"

"Miguel Cruz," he blurts, apparently not needing to be reminded of what more we can do to him. "His n-name is M-Miguel Cruz."

"Now was that so hard?" Poker states, returning the scythe to its rightful place on the wall.

"J-just do it," Monty begs. "K-kill me and get it o-over with."

"As you wish," I say, taking the three green pills Poker hands me. I shove them into Monty's mouth and cringe when his saliva coats my fingers. "It won't be long."

Monty greedily swallows the tablets, wanting death more than he wants to draw another breath. I don't blame him. The wounds inflicted upon him today would have eventually taken him, and if they didn't, Miguel Cruz certainly would.

My brother and I leave the room, letting the douchebag die alone. We'll send a prospect to clean up the mess in a few hours. As we walk through the hall, I pull out my cell to turn it back on.

"That was fun," Poker says nonchalantly, a wicked grin on his face.

"And fruitful," I remind him. "Crow's gonna be happy, that's for sure."

"Yeah. Have you ever heard of this Miguel Cruz guy?"

"No. I'm guessing he's tied to the cartel or something."

"Probably." Poker rubs his hands together. "Let's go fill in Pres, and then we—"

"Fuck!" I shout, stopping in my tracks.

"What?" he asks, turning around to face me.

I hold up my cell. "Ember's called four times and texted me that there's a problem," I explain as I tap the screen to return her call. She answers on the first ring as if she was sitting there, waiting for me to call. "What's wrong?" I growl, putting the call on speaker.

"Where have you been?" she demands, but there's more fear in her tone than anger.

"I'm sorry, Em. I had my phone off while Poker and I handled something."

"Someone came to the house, Ghost," she says. "They left a note, and it, well, it scared me. I'm sure I'm overreacting, but I thought you should know."

"I'm on my way." I glance at Poker, and he nods, somehow knowing what I need without me asking. "Poker's gonna come with me. We'll be there as soon as we can."

"Okay. Um, thanks, Ghost."

It's on the tip of my tongue to tell her she has nothing to thank me for. I'll always come when she needs me. Always. But I don't say that. I can't say that. I *won't* say that.

"Keep the doors locked, and I'll see you soon."

After she agrees, I disconnect the call and take the steps up to the main level of the clubhouse two at a time. Poker follows, calling Crow to fill him in so we don't have to stop and chat before leaving. By the time we reach our Harleys outside, we're both ready for whatever awaits us at my mom's house.

The ride seems to take twice as long as usual, and

only when we pull into the driveway does my heart no longer feel like it's going to pound out of my chest. I unlock the front door and burst inside, Poker hot on my heels. When I spot my mom sitting on the couch, knitting and watching something on TV, I skid to a halt.

"Parker West," she chides. "What are you doing running in here like your pants are on fire?"

Poker tries and fails to stifle a laugh, and I glare at him before responding. "I,uh, wanted to—"

"I asked him to come, Mrs. West," Ember says as she enters the living room. "You were wondering why he hadn't been by so I thought you might like to see him."

Mom seems to consider that for a moment. "It's a little late for a visit, sweetheart," she tells me. "I wish you'd have come earlier. I was about to go to bed."

"Sorry, Mom," I say. "I couldn't get here any earlier."

"We were helping out at the clinic," Poker lies. "Jackyl was offering flu shots tonight and needed our assistance with crowd control."

Mom laughs lightly. "I'm so proud of you boys, always doing what you can to help out the community."

"Thank you, Mrs. West," Poker says. "Hey, would you mind if I watch the end of this show with you?

It's been so long since I've been able to just sit with a pretty lady."

Mom blushes. "Oh, stop it."

Ember smothers a smile. "I'm going to go fix the guys a plate of spaghetti," she says to my mom. "I'm sure they're both hungry."

"I'll help," I say, crossing the room toward her.

"Okay, dear," Mom says, her attention on Poker and the TV.

"Show me the note," I demand the moment Ember and I are out of earshot of the others.

She reaches into her back pocket and pulls out a piece of paper to hand me. I open it, read the words, and fury slithers beneath my skin. Unsigned, it would be easy for my mind to race with possibilities about the sender, but only one name comes to mind after what Poker and I learned: Miguel Cruz.

"Who left this?" I ask her, hoping like hell I'm wrong.

Ember shrugs. "I have no clue. There was a knock on the door while we were eating dinner, but by the time I answered it, no one was there. That was taped to the door."

I snap a picture of the note and send it to Crow, giving him a heads-up on what I'm dealing with. He quickly responds.

> Crow: What the fuck?

> Me: My thoughts exactly. I'm bringing Mom and Em back to the clubhouse

> Crow: I'll have two of the rooms made up for them

> Me: Thanks, bro

I return my attention back to Ember, and she's fidgeting with her hands. "I want you to pack a bag for you and one for Mom. I think it's best if you both stay at the clubhouse for a while."

She shakes her head. "We can't do that."

"Why not?" I bark. "It's not safe here."

"You don't even know who left that," she argues. "Besides, switching up your mom's routine, forcing her to go somewhere that isn't familiar, would be detrimental for her. It wouldn't be fair and could very likely send her on a downward spiral."

Shit!

"Okay." I shove a hand through my hair and begin to pace. "You're right. I won't do that to her. But I can't leave you two here alone, not now."

"Why not? I'm a big girl, Ghost. I can keep us safe."

I bark out a laugh, but there's no humor in it.

"Em, I have no doubt of your ability to protect yourself… against normal assholes. But I have a bad feeling about this. This is about the club, and that means it's no normal asshole we're dealing with."

"Well, we can't go to the clubhouse, so I suggest you come up with another plan."

"Why don't you stay here, Ghost?" I whirl around at Poker's voice and arch a brow. "Your mom dozed off. Figured I'm more useful in here than watching her sleep."

"Right. Nosy bastard," I mutter.

"Look, I saw the note. Crow already sent it out to all of us, wanting to give us a heads up." Poker moves to sit at the table. "It makes sense that you would stay here. You can keep an eye on them and handle any threats that might pop up. It's not like you need to be at the clubhouse twenty-four-seven."

"True," I agree. "Think Crow will go for it?"

He shrugs. "Don't see why not."

"Wait a minute," Ember says, moving to the fridge to pull out leftovers. "You're seriously gonna move back home, all because of some stupid note?"

"You did say that it scared you," I remind her.

"Well, yeah, I did, but…" She gnaws on her lower lip while she prepares a plate of spaghetti for Poker and me.

"But nothing," I insist when she doesn't finish her

thought. "I'll move back in here until I know for sure that Mom and you aren't in any danger. Hopefully, it'll only be for a few days."

"And if it's not?" she asks.

I grin. "Then I guess we'll finally get to live together like we were supposed to."

CHAPTER 20
EMBER

I MISSED YOU.

"ANYTHING ELSE?"

Ghost takes the duffel from Ben and opens the zipper. Crow ordered him to bring Ghost clothes and stuff he'll need, and the prospect seems to have thought of everything. My ex pulls a box of rubbers out of the bag and frowns. He definitely won't needing those.

"Nope," Ghost says. "Should be good for now."

"Okay. I'll be on my way then." Ben moves to the door. "Have a good night."

Once the decision was made for Ghost to stay here, he didn't waste any time. It's only been an hour since then, and while his mom went to bed, happy to have her 'baby boy under the same roof again', I've been sitting on the couch wariness taking a toll on my senses.

"You, too."

Ben leaves, and Ghost drops the duffel to the floor near the hallway. Poker left once Crow gave the okay for him to go, and now that we're alone together, nerves attack my system.

"Is this really necessary?" I ask when the silence stretches on too long.

"Oh, c'mon, it won't be that bad."

When he sits, I stand. "That's exactly what I'm worried about."

The way his brows shoot up tells me I couldn't shock him more if I told him I'm a princess of some faraway country. He leans back against the cushions, appearing to weigh my words.

"Why does that worry you, Em?"

Throwing up my arms, I turn to face him. "The truth?" He doesn't bother responding because he knows that I know he always wants the truth from me. "Fine. It worries me because I'm afraid to realize that I made a huge mistake letting you go."

His mouth drops open. Apparently, I could shock him more. My earlier thoughts regarding talking to him about the last fifteen years crowd my brain. I know it's a conversation that needs to happen, but where do I even start?

"Em, come sit down," he urges, and then he waits for me to listen. I hesitate for a moment before circling the coffee table and sitting on the opposite end of the sofa. "Would it be so bad to realize it was a mistake? Do you hate me that much?"

"God, no. I don't hate you. I never did. I tried, but hating you isn't in my DNA. It's an impossibility."

"Good to know," he says, a smile in his voice. "Talk to me. Please."

I grab a throw pillow and hug it to my chest to keep myself from scooting closer to him. Talking had never been a problem between us. He was my best friend, and I could always tell him anything. Now, though… I just don't know.

"Why didn't you fight for me?" I finally ask, blurting out the one question I've always needed an answer to.

"What?"

"You didn't fight for me, Parker." He doesn't correct my use of his legal name. "I broke things off, I know, but I'd have caved. I'd have gone to Oregon with you if you wanted me to."

"I did want you to," he whispers harshly. "How could you possibly think otherwise?"

I shrug. "You never asked. You just assumed."

"We were engaged, Em," he reminds me.

"Engaged and ready to spend our lives together. I shouldn't have had to ask you to go with me."

He's right, of course. He shouldn't have had to, but I was young and dumb and, at the time, it's what I needed from him. I don't say that, though. Instead, I ask another question.

"Did you know that I called you? A week after I broke it off, I called, but you'd already moved. Why'd you leave so fast?"

He groans, as if my admission causes him physical pain. "I couldn't stay, Em. I couldn't face you, couldn't face all the questions and looks of pity from the people in this town. I had to go because if I stayed, I don't know what would've happened to me."

"When your mom told me you left, it broke me," I admit, tears springing to my eyes. "All I could picture was you in another state, living your dream, living it up… without me." I rub my chest, my heart aching. "It broke me, Parker. Shattered me into a million little pieces that took years to put back together."

He leans forward, resting his forearms on his knees, and turns his head to stare at me. Pain bleeds from his eyes, and that threatens to break me all over again.

"I wasn't living it up," he says quietly. "Hell, I was barely living at all."

I take a deep breath, and then another and another. "I'm sorry," I whisper, tears spilling over my lashes to run down my cheeks. "I'm so fucking sorry."

His carefully crafted control snaps. He moves closer and pulls me into his arms. I could struggle, but I don't want to. I need this, need him. Even if it is only temporary.

"Fuck, Em, I'm sorry, too," he says, pressing his cheek to the top of my head. I'm straddling him now, and my cheek is pressed to his chest. "So much wasted time."

I don't know how long we sit like this, me crying and him offering comfort. Eventually, my tears dry up, and I lean back to look him in the eyes.

"I missed you," I admit. "There were so many times I wanted to call, so many things I ached to tell you."

Ghost cups my cheeks and presses a soft kiss to my lips. "I missed you too. So goddamn much."

Resting my forehead against his, I ask, "Can we be friends? Can we move past all the hurt and be more than employer slash employee?"

He hesitates, and for a split second, I worry that

he'll say no, but when he replies, all my worry is chased away and replaced by warmth and relief.

"I'd love that, Em. More than you know."

CHAPTER 21
GHOST

My girl. My Em.

"We'll be fine, I promise."

Ember stands near the front door, a concerned expression etched on her face while I talk to Anna, the clinic nurse Jackyl suggested we get to stay with Mom so we could have a night off. Anna is more than capable of handling things here at the house, I know that, but I'm not the one who needs convincing.

"I know," I say, glancing at Em. "If you need anything, though, you know how to get a hold of me, right?"

"Oh, would the two of you just go," Mom says from her perch on the couch. "Anna and I will be just fine, won't we dear?"

"Yes, Mrs. West," Anna agrees.

"See?" Mom says. "Go have fun. You deserve it."

It's been almost a week since the note arrived at the house, and I moved back in. Six days have come and gone since Ember and I talked about our past and agreed we'd be friends. We've settled into a comfortable routine, one I imagine we would've settled into years ago had we not parted ways, but I refuse to dwell on that anymore. The past is just that, the past. It needs to stay where it belongs if there's any hope for a future.

I fucking want a future with Ember. But friends first.

"Unless you want me to change my mind," Ember begins. "I suggest we go."

Not too long ago, the edge in her tone would've set me off, but not now. She's worried about my mom, and that's just one of the things I love about her.

Love?

Fuck, yes, love. Now that I've had time to process what went down, how we both felt afterward, I've realized that I never stopped loving her. Accepting that has made things so much clearer. Like why I've never found another woman to settle down with or why I gravitated to undercover work as a cop. It required no attachments, demanded it. It was easy.

"Okay, we're going. Anna, call if you need anything," I say again.

"I will."

Ember and I walk outside, and anticipation fills me as we near my Harley. She's the only girl to ever ride on the back of my bike, and I can't wait to feel her thighs squeezing me, her arms wrapped around my waist.

"I haven't been on a bike in forever," she says, smiling wistfully at the machine.

"Good to know," I say with a smirk. "C'mon." I grab her hand and help her onto the seat before settling in front of her.

"Don't wreck," she teases.

"With you on the back? Never."

The ride to the clubhouse is heaven and Hell all at the same time. Having her pressed so close, her breasts smashed against my back, was the best torture. What I wouldn't give to have her naked, squirming beneath me, writhing in pleasure.

After parking in front of the clubhouse, I help her off the Harley, and she wobbles a little. "It *has* been a while, hasn't it?"

She laughs nervously. "Yep. Gimme a minute."

"No problem."

Music fills the air, as well as laughter from inside.

The party is in full swing. It's not an open party where outsiders are welcome, other than Ember of course, which is good because I didn't want to overwhelm her.

"What if they don't like me?" she asks, her voice cutting through my thoughts.

"They're gonna love you. Besides, you already know Crow and Addison. As for the rest, I'm sure you'll recognize some from town."

"Knowing and recognizing someone doesn't mean they'll like me."

"You worry too much."

She scrunches her nose. "Probably."

I grab her hand and tug her inside, deciding that we need to treat this like ripping off a Band-Aid. The quicker, the better.

"Ember!" Crow shouts as soon as we step over the threshold. He makes his way toward us and wraps her in a hug before she can stop him. "It's about time this asshat let you out for a night of fun."

And just like that, her nervousness vanishes. She laughs, and it's genuine this time, not tinged with a hint of apprehension.

"He's a harsh taskmaster, isn't he?" she counters, grinning at Pres.

Blood rushes to my cock at her words. Okay, fine, only one word triggers my reaction: master.

I've never considered myself dominant or a man who needs their woman to be submissive, but maybe I should try it out. My dick certainly wants me to.

"He's a big ol' softy," Addison chimes in when she joins us.

"Hey, now," I chide. "Watch it."

"Says the man scolding *my* old lady," Crow snarls, taking a step closer to me.

"Down, boy," Addison says, patting him on the chest. "I can handle Ghost."

Crow grunts then turns his attention back to Ember. "Make yourself at home, have a few drinks, meet the brothers. We can catch up later."

Sometimes I forget that Crow and Ember have known each other as long as he and I have. We all grew up in Marble Falls, as did Addison, but we didn't always run in the same circles.

"Thanks," Em says.

"C'mon, I'll introduce you to the rest of 'em."

I lead her toward the bar where Journey is sitting with his old lady, Wren. Silently, I send up a prayer that Wren is actually Wren and not one of her alters. I still haven't figured out who is who.

"You must be Ember," Journey greets when we reach them. "I'm Journey, VP of all these bastards."

"Nice to meet you."

"I'm Wren." She thrusts her hand out to shake

Ember's. "His better half," she continues, tilting her head to indicate Journey.

"Nice to meet you, too," Ember says as I release a breath I didn't realize I was holding. She glances at me. "What's wrong with you?"

"He was worried that he wouldn't know who I was," Wren says, saving me from answering. When Ember looks at her with confusion wrinkling her forehead, Wren explains. "I've got dissociative identity disorder, or multiple personalities. I'm pretty good at recognizing triggers and avoiding them, thanks to therapy and medication, but sometimes one of the twelve will pop out of nowhere and fuck with the people around me."

"Twelve?" Ember asks.

"Yep. Aren't I a lucky girl?" Wren teases, able to joke about it now that she's found love with my brother.

"I have so many questions, but I'll refrain… for now." Ember grins. "Something tells me you've got stories."

She and Wren talk for a few minutes longer, and Journey and I simply watch and soak up the fact that our girls are getting along so well.

Our girls. My girl. My Em.

Because it's not an open party, it doesn't take long

to introduce her to everyone else. She's friendly with each of them, even the club whores. I should've known she would be. Ember is the embodiment of kindness and acceptance. One thing she's never been is judgmental or nasty to someone who is different from her.

Two hours later, I'm nursing my third beer, and she's on her fourth. I'm learning that she's a lightweight when it comes to alcohol, but as long as she's safe and having fun, I couldn't care less. I'm just happy she's letting loose and not worrying about my mom or that fucking note.

"Please tell me you're not gonna let her get away again."

I turn to face Crow as he takes the stool next to me, both of us watching as Ember, Addison, and Wren dance to the music.

"We're just friends."

"Bro, your lips say one thing, but your eyes say something else entirely."

I arch a brow. "And what do they say, oh wise one?"

"They're screaming 'mine'," he says, chuckling, and then his gaze shifts to the left of the girls. "Aw, shit. Better claim her before that gets outta control."

My vision blurs as I watch Python crowd Ember and wrap his arms around her waist to pull her against him. I'm off the stool and across the room in seconds, yanking him away from her.

"What the fuck do you think you're doing?" I snarl.

"Dancin', bro," he counters. "What's it look like?"

"Looks like you want my fist down your fucking throat for touching my woman," I seethe, gripping his cut and getting in his face.

"Didn't know you'd claimed her."

Of course, he didn't. Because I haven't.

Fuck.

"Um, Ghost," Ember says, her voice registering through the haze of rage. She rests her hand on my chest, trying to urge me away from Python, and I let her, dropping my arms. "He didn't do anything wrong."

"Bullshit," I snap. "He touched you."

"Okay, but—"

"But nothing." I lift her into my arms, and she wraps her legs around my hips. "You're mine, Em," I growl possessively. "You hear me? Mine."

Her tongue darts out to wet her lips, and she squirms against me. My cock thickens, and I'm so horny that I could fuck her right here, right now. But she's drunk.

"I'm yours," she says softly.

"Hear that, everyone?" I shout to be heard over

the thumping bass. "Ember's mine. Touch her and answer to me."

Cheers erupt around us, but I ignore them. The only person existing in my orbit now that I've made my declaration is the woman in my arms.

"I thought we were just friends," she says as I carry her out of the main room toward my bedroom.

Her statement causes my steps to falter. "Is that really what you want?"

Ember rocks her hips. "Right now, I wanna get naked with you."

Groaning, I shake my head. "Em, I want that too, but not like this."

"Like what?"

"You're drunk," I point out. "I refuse to take advantage of that, no matter how much I crave you."

"It's not taking advantage if I want it too."

We reach my room, and after setting her on the bed, I lock the door. I shove my hands through my hair, trying like hell to hold on to every ounce of my control. When I turn back around to face her, my mouth waters.

"Like what you see?" she taunts, kneeling on the mattress, naked as the day she was born.

I shove my hands in my pockets. "Love it," I croak.

"Take what you want, Ghost. Please."

At least she didn't say 'fuck me'. I don't think I'd have been able to resist that. But taking what I want… That I can do.

I quickly strip and join her on the bed. Pulling her down to lie in the crook of my arm, I yank the blanket up to cover us and then kiss her shoulder.

"Sleep, Em," I whisper. "I want you to sleep."

CHAPTER 22
EMBER

We can do that.

The pounding in my head wakes me up, and I roll over as my stomach pitches. Fortunately, I don't puke because the last thing I want to do is clean up a mess. An arm settles on my side, startling me, and my eyes fly open.

"You okay?"

Ghost?

"Um…" Cotton coats my tongue, and I try to swallow past the thickness. "No."

He chuckles and sits up to lean over and stare into my eyes. "You didn't even drink that much."

I narrow my eyes. "Asshole."

His face disappears for a moment and then

returns, his grin still present. I'd like to slap that grin away, but I'm afraid if I move too much, I'll die.

"Here," he says, handing me a glass of water and two Tylenol. I shake my head, instantly regretting it. "It'll help, Em."

"Can't sit up," I mumble. "Too hard."

He slides an arm under my back to ease me into a sitting position. My stomach rolls, and I slap a hand to my mouth.

"Breathe," he urges. "In through your nose, out through your mouth." I follow his lead, and the nausea abates. "Better?"

"Little bit." I take the water and wash down the Tylenol with a small sip. My head clears slightly, and I glance around before my eyes land on him… specifically, his bare chest. "Uh…"

"Nothing happened," he assures me. "You got naked and were very tempting, but all we did was sleep."

"Right."

"How much *did* I drink last night?" I ask, afraid of the answer.

"You only had four beers," he tells me. "You used to be able to tolerate more than that."

"What about the shots? How many of those did I have?"

It had to be quite a few because I don't recall a time I've ever been this hungover.

"You didn't have any."

"I did, though. I know Addison gave me a few." I squint as I try to recall who else handed me shot glasses throughout the night. "I'm sure there was more, but I can't remember who gave them to me."

Ghost tenses beside me. "I must've missed it," he snarls, and I lean into him in an effort to calm him down.

"It's okay," I assure him. "It's not like anyone forced me to drink."

"It's not okay," he insists. "I should've paid more attention."

"You can't watch me every second," I scoff.

His scowl turns to a grin. "I sure as fuck want to."

Rolling my eyes, I scoot to the edge of the bed and set my feet on the floor. Just then, a memory slams into me, and I stiffen. "Did you threaten one of your brothers last night?" I ask, glancing over my shoulder.

"Maybe."

"Yes or no?"

"Yes." He scratches the side of his nose. "Python had it coming though."

More of the incident surfaces in my mind. "Oh

my God," I say on a whoosh of breath. "You told them all that I belonged to you."

"I did." There's not the slightest bit of apology or regret in his tone.

Not that I want there to be.

"Why?"

Ghost shifts on the mattress so he's sitting behind me and slides his arms over my shoulders. "Em, I know we're just supposed to be friends, honestly, I do. But…"

My heart stutters. "But what?"

"What if we're meant to be more?"

"What if we're not?"

He sighs, releasing me so he can move to stand in front of me. "Em, look at me."

I lift my eyes to his. "I'm scared."

"Fuck, I am, too. But I think it's worth a shot. *We're* worth a shot."

"This is crazy."

He grabs my hand and pulls me to my feet. "Embrace the crazy with me, Em."

I can't stop the tilt of my lips. I want to embrace it, embrace him. It's not like we're strangers, not really. I've tried to fill the void left after breaking up with him, and the only thing that came close to making me whole again was work, always work.

"We can't go back to what we were before," I say.

"No, we can't," he agrees. "We were broken before. I don't want that any more than you do."

"And we have to take things slow because… well, just because."

"I can do slow." He must sense my continued hesitation because he continues. "Em, forget about labels, about the past or what the future might hold. Just think about this, us, right here, right now. We'll take it one day at a time. No expectations. We'll simply be together in whatever way feels right in the moment."

That is why no one has ever compared to this man. He gets me on a level that others don't even bother to try for. And it's exactly why I'm going to give in.

"Okay. I can do that. We can do that."

CHAPTER 23
GHOST

Fingers crossed.

"See you later."

I kiss Ember on the cheek before leaving to head back to the clubhouse. Anna needed to get to work at the clinic, so Em was needed with my mom.

"I won't be late," I promise.

Listen to me, sounding all domestic. We agreed not to define what's between us, and here I am, talking to her as if she's my old lady.

She should've been. She still will be.

I return to the clubhouse just in time for church to start. As soon as I take my seat, Crow calls the meeting to order.

"Okay, brothers," he begins. "As you all know, we've got the name of the prick killing our people and stealing our brand. I wanna take him down as quickly as possible so this shit stops." He nods at Tracer. "Give them whatever you were able to dig up."

"Miguel Cruz is from Sinaloa, Mexico," Tracer informs. "Thirty-one, unmarried, and from what I can gather, unattached. I've found several things indicating that he may have children by three different women, but I haven't been able to corroborate with birth certificates. He doesn't pay child support or anything like that, at least not that's on public record." Tracer glances at his laptop, the only electronic permitted in church, other than Crow's cell. "He's been arrested numerous times for drug offenses but never served any time. He's got a cousin in the cartel so I'm sure that's how he manages to get off. Based on all reports I've been able to find, he's moved up to Texas from Sinaloa to cultivate his own drug operation. Looks like he's trying to impress the cartel, garner more favor from them."

"In other words, he's a dangerous man who wants to make a name for himself among even more dangerous men," I say dryly. I wish I was surprised, but the drug business never changes no matter what side you're on.

"Exactly."

"This fucker's gotta go," Fudge barks. "No way can he make a name for himself here."

"Certainly not a good one," Screamer agrees.

"Which is why we're here," Crow snaps. "We've gotta get this guy out of our fucking territory. Shit, I'd be happier if he was dead, but I'll settle for gone if I have to."

"Any idea where he's hiding himself?" Python asks Tracer.

"Sort of. I can't find an address, but I used facial recognition to go through all known security cameras in Marble Falls and he popped up on a video feed near the bank on Main Street."

"Has he been there more than once?" Journey asks.

"Every Monday morning at ten," Tracer confirms.

"If we follow him from there, we should be able to track him back to his hidey-hole," I say. "We can take him out there."

Crow shakes his head. "We need to get info out of him first. The way I see it, we've got two options. One is that we follow him home from the bank and snatch him up to bring him to the Nightmare Room."

"I like that option," Stunner says, a sinister grin on his face.

"I agree," Fudge adds. "But we don't know who

or what he's got at his place. We could be walking into a death trap."

"What's option two?" I ask, wanting to get every possible angle out on the table to analyze. They all already know about the note, so I don't bother mentioning it again. But it's what's driving me, driving my desperation to stop Cruz no matter what. He scared Em, and I can't let that slide.

"Rather than follow him anywhere, we pick up one of his lackeys and have them deliver a message to meet us at a place of our choosing, a place we can control, and grill him there."

"As much as I want Cruz to bleed," Tracer says. "I think option two is the best. There's nothing saying we can't still take him out, but this gives all of us the best chance at survival."

"I second that," Fudge says.

"Me too," Python adds.

"Agreed," Journey states.

"Okay, I get it," Crow says with a chuckle. "All in favor of option two, thump twice."

Each of us pounds the table two times in quick succession. For the rest of the afternoon, we strategize. It won't be hard to locate another of Cruz's dealers… Unfortunately, they're everywhere. And if there's anything a Soulless King can do, it's to force a person to do what we want them to do.

By the time church ends, I'm more than ready to return to my mom's house. But I have some things to do first.

Now that I'm staying at the house, Ember and I haven't talked about how she wants to handle her days off. If it were my call to make, all of her free time would be spent with me. I want to get to know her, the woman she is now. I want to learn what makes her tick, what makes her smile, what makes her cry, and what scares her.

In order to do that, we're going to need time together without Mom. Which is why I plan on surprising Ember tonight with a date of sorts. In order to accomplish it, I have errands to run and supplies to buy. I know it'll be worth it in the end, and I hope like hell she agrees.

Fingers crossed.

CHAPTER 24
EMBER

What a way to go.

"I hope you know what you're doing."

"Me too," I reply, wedging my cell between my shoulder and ear.

Lori and I have been talking for only a few minutes, and I didn't waste any time telling her about my agreement with Ghost to take things a day at a time. At the moment, I'm second-guessing the decision.

Ghost told me he wouldn't be late, and it's already after nine. He texted me around five and said he had some things to do but that I shouldn't eat dinner. I'm hungry and cranky and getting tired.

Where is he?

"Earth to Ember," Lori says, yanking me from my thoughts. "What's going on in that head of yours?"

"What? Nothing, why?"

"Because you got super quiet all of a sudden."

"Oh. I was just thinking."

"About him?"

I can't stop the giggle that escapes, making me sound like a naive schoolgirl. "Always."

"Promise me one thing," she says.

"Anything."

"Be careful."

"Trust me, Lor, I will. The last thing I want is another broken heart. I know I won't survive it this time around."

My phone beeps with an incoming call, and I glance at the screen to see Ghost's name flash. "Hey, I gotta go. He's calling."

"Okay. Call me tomorrow."

"Will do." I switch calls. "Hi."

"Hey, Em." There's a smile in his voice. "I know it's late, and I'm sorry about that, but I need you to do me a favor."

"What favor?" I ask suspiciously.

"First, is Mom in bed?"

"Yeah. She went in about eight-thirty. It was a rough day, and she was exhausted."

"Damn. Okay, well, at least we won't be interrupted."

"Ghost, what are you talking about? What favor? What won't be interrupted."

"Favor first. I need you to go to the backyard."

"Okay. I'm going."

Grateful I decided not to change into my pajamas, I stand from the bed and walk through the house. When I reach the door to the back deck, the blind is closed. I don't recall closing it earlier but shrug it off.

"Where are you?" I ask as I wrap my hand around the knob and twist.

I push the door open and almost drop my cell. Ghost is standing on the deck, a bouquet of lilies in his hand and a shit-eating grin on his lips. He lowers his cell and shoves it in his pocket.

"I'm right here."

"What is this?"

"Well, I figured we deserved a proper date, but since we can't leave Mom, this is the next best thing."

Ghost reaches for my hand and tugs me across the deck and down the steps to the yard. There's a firepit I know for a fact wasn't there before, and crackling flames light up the space. He's also set up a small table for two, complete with candles, a chilling bottle of wine, and two covered plates that remind me of what you get when you order room service at a hotel.

Tears spring to my eyes. "You did all this?"

He nods. "It's why I'm late. I'm sorry about that, by the way."

I shake my head frantically. "It's okay. I can't believe you did this."

In the firelight, his eyes sparkle, and I can see the blush across his cheeks. "I wanted to do something nice for you. To show you how much I appreciate what you've taken on with Mom, and how much I appreciate… *you*."

"Thank you."

"I hope you're hungry because there's a veritable feast under those domes," he says.

He pulls my chair out for me, and I sit. Next he reveals the food, and he wasn't joking about it being a feast. We each have a steak, baked potato, mixed vegetables, a dinner roll, and a piece of peanut butter pie.

"This looks delicious."

As if on cue, my stomach rumbles, causing us both to laugh.

"Let's eat. I'm ready for what comes after." He winks at me.

The conversation is easy as we consume our meals, almost as if we never spent any time apart. We reminisce about old times, never even touching on the breakup or anything painful. With Ghost, I can be myself because it's easy, it's natural.

"Now for the second act," he teases, gripping my hand and helping me to my feet when we're done eating.

"Oh, man," I say, my hand on my stomach. "I think you're gonna have to give me a bit before any activities."

"Get your mind outta the gutter."

I arch a brow. "Oh, so it's not sex that you were referring to?"

"Nope." He grins. "Not yet, anyway."

"Okay, then what's next?"

Ghost takes out his cell and taps the screen a few times until there's slow music playing. Then he eases me into his arms and starts to sway.

"Now, we dance," he whispers in my ear. "When I saw Python put his hands around you, doing what I wanted to do, it made me crazy. It's my turn."

I shiver at his words, at his touch. He traces lazy circles over my lower back, and between him and the fire, I'm hypnotized. Every touch sends tiny little zings through me, each one ending between my legs. After a while, my knees start to weaken, and I'm desperate to have him, all of him.

"As fun as this is," I begin, my voice shaking a little. "I want more. I *need* more."

Without hesitation, he lowers me to the ground, and I realize I missed the blanket he placed there. It's soft and protects us both from the dewy grass.

"You are so fucking beautiful, Em," he says with reverence as he slides my shirt off my shoulder to press kisses to my collarbone. "Especially here, where you're inked. Sexy as hell." I shiver beneath him. "I'm gonna strip you bare and take my time with you."

"Mmmm," I moan. "Please."

The cool air causes my flesh to pebble with goosebumps when the last stitch of clothing disappears. Ghost caresses my sides, moving until the tips of his fingers barely graze my nipples. They harden under his touch, and I'm lost.

"You were always so responsive to me." He moves for a moment, and I immediately miss his heat. But when I hear rustling clothes, I know he'll return to me naked, and the missing will be worth it. "Feel what you do to me," he coaxes as he settles on top of me, his hard cock pressing against my pelvis. "Fucking granite."

"Inside," I plead. "Need you inside."

"Not yet."

Ghost slides down my body and pushes my

thighs apart, opening me for him. His tongue circles my clit, and I buck my hips, desperation driving me. He inserts one finger, using my desire to ease his way, and then he adds a second. Curling his digits inside of me, he hits that elusive spot that only he's ever been able to find and increases the flicks of his tongue.

I shatter around him, the orgasm taking me by surprise in its intensity. Ghost doesn't slow his movements until my legs stop quivering and my uneven pants settle into a more normal breathing pattern.

When he straightens, he licks his fingers clean while maintaining eye contact. And it's hot as fuck.

I reach for his cock, wrapping my fingers around his thick length, and he goes rigid. "Now," I purr. "Inside me, now."

Guiding him to my entrance, I remove my hand when he pushes his head in. And when he stops, it takes everything in me not to slap him.

"Please, Parker," I beg. "Please don't stop."

He lowers his head, sealing his lips to mine, and holy God he moves. Sparks light me up from the inside out as he thrusts in and out, the drag of his dick intoxicating. Part of me wants to demand he move faster, fuck me harder, but the rest of me wants exactly what he's offering. Slow, sweet, perfect.

Never breaking the kiss, he slides his arm under

me to arch my back, and it changes the angle enough to turn the sparks into full blown flames. I'm on fire, burning for him.

"Come for me, Em," he says against my lips. "Come around my cock."

His words tip me over the edge, and his body goes rigid as his own orgasm barrels into him. The pulsing of his release drags mine out to the point I fear it'll kill me.

What a way to go, though.

After a blissful eternity, we both relax, and he rolls to my side. I pillow my cheek on his chest and flatten my palm over his rapidly beating heart.

"I needed that," I tell him, my eyelids beginning to droop.

"*We* needed that."

"Hmmm."

"Sleep, Em. I'll carry you inside in a bit. For now, I just want to hold you."

"'Kay," I reply drowsily, giving up the fight.

As we lay there, Ghost's arms are around me like I'm the sweetest treasure. And at the moment sleep drags me under, I swear I hear him say he loves me.

I love you, too.

CHAPTER 25
GHOST

I VOW TO BRING HELL TO ANYONE WHO DARES LAY A FINGER ON MY MOM OR EMBER.

A month later...

"You'll be careful, right?"

The worry in Ember's eyes threatens to take me to my knees. There've been no more threats to her or my mom, but the club managed to get a message to Cruz, and the meeting with him goes down tonight. This is the first time I've had to leave her, leave them, for something this dangerous.

"I'm always careful, Em," I tell her, resting my arms on her shoulders.

I haven't returned to the clubhouse, and she and I are now sharing a room, much to Mom's delight. We've come a long way since that first phone call a few months ago. Neither of us hide from our feelings, and we talk about everything and anything. We also agreed that we never end a day angry or with questions or doubts.

"I know you are," she says. "But this is club business, and I know that, more often than not, that means your safety is at risk."

"I'll never lie to you and tell you that I'm never in danger." I stroke her cheek. "Just know that I will always do whatever it takes to get back to you. And the guys have my back. I'm not going alone."

She nods. "I know."

I wait for her to say more, ask me questions, but she doesn't which makes her even more perfect for me. Ember knows that I will always have secrets, but she trusts that I'll never hold something back that affects her. After a long discussion with Crow, Journey, and Jackyl, the married brothers, I learned that's how it's done. Em is good with the compromise.

"I love you," I say, kissing her.

"I love you, too."

The rumble of Harleys breaks us apart, and I glance out the window to see Journey, Jackyl, Screamer, Fudge, and Ben pull up in the driveway.

"I gotta go," I say. "Ben will be outside until I get back, okay? You and Mom won't be left unprotected."

"I know. And we'll be fine. You just worry about you."

Despite all being quiet as far as threats go, it was agreed that tonight of all nights, someone needed to be here just in case.

"I'll text you as soon as I'm done and on my way home."

"You better."

I grin. "Kiss me again."

She does, sweeping her tongue past the seam of my lips. I'm rock hard in an instant, and it would be so easy to ignore the men outside, but I can't. I won't.

"Let's go!" Journey shouts from outside, breaking us apart.

When I step onto the porch, I wait to go farther until Ember locks the front door. Satisfied that she and Mom, who's already gone to bed, will be safe, I jog down the steps and hop on my Harley.

"'Bout time," Python grumbles. "I was starting to worry your dick was glued to her pussy or something."

I ignore the jibe. He's been doing everything he can to joke about me and Ember, I'm guessing in an effort to remind me that he's fully aware that she's taken. It's

Those of us with a patch take off, and Ben stays behind, staying with his bike in the driveway. Ember will invite him in, I'm sure, but he won't accept. He can keep a better watch from where he's at than if he goes in and gets comfortable.

It takes twenty minutes to arrive at the agreed upon location, and we park next to motorcycles of the brothers already here. I take in the black Rolls-Royce Ghost with its Black Badge package and roll my eyes.

Cruz certainly isn't subtle, but I doubt this is a daily driver for him. People in Marble Falls would definitely have noticed something this flashy. It's more likely he breaks it out when he wants his enemies to think he's got the bigger dick.

"I hate to admit it, but that's a cage I wouldn't mind riding in," Jackyl states, adjusting himself.

"It's fucking gorgeous," Screamer agrees.

"The fucker's here early," Journey snaps. Cruz wasn't supposed to arrive for another twenty minutes or so. "Let's get inside."

We follow our VP, and the sound of voices reaches my ears. There's no shouting, so that's a good sign. When we reach the larger room, Crow, Tracer, Poker, and Stunner are standing in a line, facing who I assume is Miguel. He's got two men flanking him on either side as well.

"You're late," Crow barks. To anyone who doesn't know him, they'd think him pissed, but he's not. He simply wants to make sure that Cruz and his cronies know that he's in charge.

"They're early," Journey states, nodding at the enemy.

"Yes, we are," Cruz says matter-of-factly, his accent thick. "My men were getting rather anxious to get this over with, so we took a chance." He shrugs. "You were here, so all is well."

"That's where you're wrong," Crow says casually as we join them across from Cruz. "All is not fucking well. Not even close."

"Ah, yes, so your message said." Cruz grins, but it doesn't reach his eyes. "Something about Marble Falls being your territory, I believe. Please, explain."

"As you said, Marble Falls belongs to the Soulless Kings," Crow begins. "We don't tolerate anyone trying to encroach."

"My apologies. All you had to do was say so. I'm sure we can come to an arrangement that will be beneficial to us both."

"Your apologies don't mean shit," Poker snarls. "This goes way beyond encroachment. You're stealing our brand, selling it as your own, and killing people."

"That is the drug business, is it not?" Cruz asks.

"Maybe it is in Sinaloa," Crow says, and Cruz's eyes flash fury. "Yes, we know where you're from.

We also know you're trying to impress the cartel, but you can't do that here. Not on our turf."

Cruz glances at the man on his right. "Did you hear that Fernando? They have information on me."

Fernando smiles sinisterly. "Seems like they do."

"Should I be worried?"

Fernando shrugs. "I don't believe so. We've got info on them as well."

Not surprising, considering the note.

"I don't care what you think you have," Crow snarls. "I care about what you're gonna do."

"Oh?" Cruz crosses his arms over his chest like he doesn't have a care in the world. "And what are we going to do?"

"You're going to round up all the pills you've got floating around out there and leave Marble Falls. I'll be generous and give you twenty-four hours."

"Is that right?"

Crow looks from him to Journey and back again. "Yeah, that's right."

"Before I agree to that, I think you might be interested in a few things."

"Sure, why not? I'll listen."

Cruz takes a step forward. "You're married to a one Addison McGill, and boy was she a hard one to win over considering she was the police chief's daughter." He turns to Journey. "You're married to

Wren Abbot. I was very pleased to read that her therapist believes she's making great progress with those twelve pesky personalities. I can only imagine how tough that is for a girl like her." He shifts his gaze to Jackyl. "And you, club doctor, are married to Leah, Wren's friend. I like that. Keep your inner circle tight." Jackyl stiffens as Cruz turns in the opposite direction and glares at me. "And then there's you… Parker West, the wild card of the bunch. I'm not going to lie, I was worried about how things would play out with you. I mean, former undercover cop in Oregon, a long list of achievements during your years of service. Imagine my surprise when I learned that your sweet mother is battling Alzheimer's. That's rough, I know. My own abuela died from the disease… forgot to eat and wasted away. Such a sad thing. But enough about me… back to dear old Mom. It would be rather difficult for her to tell the difference between friend and foe, don't you think? Considering how her memory sometimes plays tricks on her."

"You've done your homework," I say, my voice tight, every muscle tense. "So what?"

"So," Cruz says, dragging the word out. "Do you really think a man like me only has these two men at his disposal?"

That's all it takes for chaos to ensue.

"Go!" Crow shouts at me. "Go to them!"

I take off running while gunfire explodes behind me. With each step, I vow to bring Hell to anyone who dares lay a finger on my mom or Ember. Part of me hopes that Cruz is just fucking with me, taunting me to get a reaction. But the logical part of me, the part of me that is keenly aware of the evil in the world knows that he's not.

He sent evil to my door, and I pray Ben can handle it until I get there.

CHAPTER 26
EMBER

Marry me.

I glance at my cell for the millionth time to see if I missed anything from Ghost, and groan when I realize the fucking thing is dead. Before rushing to my room to grab my charger, I stop to check on Mrs. West. I turn the knob to push open her door and lean in to look toward the bed.

Pain radiates in my head, my vision blurs, and I collapse in an unconscious heap on the floor.

When I come to, I'm tied to Mrs. West's bed, arms and legs spread out and anchored to the four posts. My head spins when I try to lift it.

"Oh, good," a man says, stepping out of the dark corner. "You're awake."

A garbled noise catches my attention, and I swivel

my head to look toward the other corner. Panic claws at my throat when I see Mrs. West tied to one of the kitchen chairs, a piece of cloth wrapped around her head to act as a gag.

"What the hell?" I mutter. "What's going on?"

"Isn't it obvious?" the man counters. "You're being held hostage."

His accent is heavy, and his eyes appear black as night.

"What do you want?" I demand, ignoring the throbbing behind my own eyes.

"That's not the question you should be asking," he taunts. "I think what you really want to know is who am I?"

"Fine, yes, that."

I'll ask him anything if it means he keeps talking and stays focused on me.

"I'm Jose Santiago."

"Great. Now what the fuck do you want?"

It's not lost on me that knowing his name isn't a benefit. If anything, it only means he'll actually kill me and Mrs. West when he's done whatever it is he came here to do.

"My boss sent me here to keep an eye on the old lady," he explains, nodding toward Ghost's mom. "You see, Mr. Cruz made it clear to me that I'm only to scare her, but he didn't mention anything about you. So, now it's my turn to ask a question. Who are *you*?"

If I weren't strapped to a bed, I'd find it mildly annoying that he doesn't know the answer to that. "Do you need to know my name to do whatever it is you're gonna do?"

"I think it would be better for you if I called you by your name instead of whore while I fuck you, don't you?" Chills race down my spine. "You see, what the boss doesn't know won't hurt him, and he definitely didn't know about you." Jose tilts his head. "Or maybe he did, and he wants me to take initiative with you."

"Touch me, and I'll kill you," I snarl, knowing full well that my binds will prevent me from doing a damn thing.

Mrs. West tries to scream, but the gag muffles the sound. Jose turns his back on me to focus on her. "Ma'am, I really need you to shut up," he snaps.

When she doesn't, he shoves the gun in his hand into his waistband, bends down, and unties her. Then he drags her out of the room. I take the time he's gone to struggle against my restraints, but it's useless. He didn't use rope, which I'd have a chance of loosening. No, he used chains, which are secured with locks.

He returns minutes later, and smirks. "That's better. Now we can enjoy each other in peace."

This guy's delusional. Seriously fucked in the head if he thinks I'm going to let any second of this be peaceful.

"You won't get away with this."

"Ah, but I will." He nods toward the doorway. "She's definitely not going to remember anything. One of the perks of her illness, right?" The question is rhetorical because he keeps talking. "And her precious son is probably dead by now so…" He shrugs, letting that tidbit hang between us.

"If you were only sent here to scare her, why would Ghost be dead?" I ask, refusing to believe that's a possibility.

"Because Mr. Cruz doesn't give a damn about Ghost or those other Soulless King fucks. He only wants to rule Marble Falls. A sick old lady isn't going to hinder his ability to do that." He closes the distance between himself and the bed. "But you are another matter. You'll talk, I'm sure. But first, I'm going to have my fun."

He grabs his gun and runs the barrel up the inside of my leg. Vomit creeps up the back of my throat, and despite my best effort, I can't stop it from spewing from my mouth.

Jose glares at me. "Disgusting," he snaps before he starts hitting me with the butt of the gun.

He strikes my face, my stomach, my legs, not missing an inch of my body. I'll be one giant bruise for sure if he keeps it up.

"Get the fuck away from me!" I shout, hating the fear in my voice.

He lands one last blow to my torso before smirking. "No, I don't think I will." Jose strips out of his clothes, tossing them to the floor. "It's a pity I had to take out that punk outside. It would've been nice to have him watch. I do like putting on a show."

Ben! I totally forgot about him.

Ghost is going to be beyond pissed when he gets here. And he is going to get here. I have to believe that, or I'd give up.

Jose pulls a pocketknife from his discarded pants and slices the blade through my shirt, exposing my breasts.

"A bit small for my taste, but I'll make do," he taunts as he drags the blade across both nipples, drawing fresh blood to mingle with the damage he's already caused.

Next, he cuts my sweats and panties away. Instinctively, I try to clench my thighs but can't. Tears fill my eyes, and no amount of wishing them gone makes it happen, so I squeeze them shut and do my best to block out every ounce of pain and what's about to happen.

Jose crawls on top of me, his nasty dick flopping against my stomach, and holds the knife to my throat. I force myself to think about Ghost and what our future would've been like. I imagine I'm on a porch swing with him, watching our kids run around the yard and catching lightning bugs in jars.

One second, my imagination is running wild, and the next, my eyes are flying open as Jose's weight leaves my body.

"You motherfucker!"

Ghost?!

I'm crying in earnest now, a mix of fear and happiness warring in my mind. I knew he'd come for me. I'd *hoped* he'd come.

Ghost and Jose roll around on the floor, each one trying to best the other. Weapons are scattered forcing them both to fight with their fists. I can barely see through my tears, but I can hear. Bone crunches, men grunt, and I swear I even hear blood splatter on the wall.

"I'll kill you for daring to touch her," Ghost growls when he gains the upper hand.

He pummels Jose's face, one blow after another, but Jose manages to roll out from under him and flip them so he's on top. Now it's Ghost's face that's getting hammered.

"Leave him alone!" I scream, yanking against the chains and ignoring the way they cut into my limbs.

What's a little more damage in the grand scheme of things?

Movement at the doorway pulls my attention away from the fight, and my eyes widen when I see Mrs. West raise a shotgun, aim it at Jose, and pull the trigger.

He collapses on top of Ghost, his head blown apart by the blast. Ghost shoves him away and scrambles to his feet, staring at his mom incredulously. He cautiously walks toward her, his hand outstretched for the gun.

"Mom, why don't you give me that, hm?" he says quietly.

She does as he asks. "He was going to kill you," she says.

"I know. You saved me."

Mrs. West's eyes find me, and her shoulders deflate. "Oh, Ember, honey." She closes the distance between us. "I'm so sorry I couldn't help you sooner."

I shake my head. "It's okay. I'm okay."

She tenderly touches my cheeks, and I wince. "You're far from okay, but you will be."

"Hey, Mom, do you think you could get me the bolt cutters from the garage?" Ghost asks. "I need to get Em free."

"Of course." She scurries off to do his bidding, no hint of the Alzheimer's that plagues her.

Ghost goes to the closet and grabs a blanket from the shelf to cover me with. "Fuck, Em, I'm so sorry I didn't get here sooner."

"You got here, that's all that matters."

His gaze travels from my battered face to my neck. "Did he…?"

"He was close, but no," I tell him.

"I swear on all that's holy, if Crow and the others haven't already killed that Cruz fuck, I will."

I laugh bitterly, which sends me into a painful coughing fit. "I'm gonna hold you to that," I say when I'm able.

Mrs. West returns, and Ghost cuts me free. He carries me out of the bedroom, wrapped up in the blanket, and as he steps outside, his brothers pull into the driveway.

"I'm taking her to the clubhouse," Ghost says. "Jackyl, meet us there."

"On it," the club doc says.

Crow helps Ghost get me situated in the back of my car and then helps Mrs. West into the passenger seat.

"Can you drive?" Ghost asks his president. "I need to stay close to her."

"Sure thing, brother."

When Ghost slides into the back seat, he cradles my head in his lap, careful not to jostle me too much.

"Em?" he whispers.

"Hmm."

"Marry me."

It's not a question, it's a plea. I open my mouth to put him out of his misery, to promise to marry him tomorrow if he wants, but before any words pass my lips, I pass out from the pain.

CHAPTER 27
GHOST

I'm not going anywhere.

"She's gonna be okay."

I glare at Jackyl, who's finishing up with Ember's stitches. Seventy-six of them to be exact. It's killing me that he's seeing her naked, but I know it's the only way for him to do his job.

"Stop it, Parker," Mom chides from the bed on the other side of the room. "She's in good hands."

Of course, she is. I wouldn't let Jackyl touch her if I thought otherwise. Doesn't change the fact that I hate everything about this entire situation.

"She'll probably sleep for a while, what with the sedative I gave her before tending to her injuries," Jackyl states. "Why don't you go get cleaned up?"

Glancing down at myself, I take in my blood-stained clothes and wince. "I'm not leaving her."

"Okay, then can I at least bring you something to change into?" he asks. "You stink, and quite frankly, if she sees you like this when she wakes up, Ember's gonna freak."

"Fine."

He turns to Mom. "Mrs. West, can I get you anything? How's your pain level?"

"No thank you, dear. And I told you, I have no pain."

When I arrived at the house earlier, I saw Ben in the driveway, gunshot wound to the chest. He was beyond help, so I raced inside to find Ember and my mom. I heard Mom first, in the bathroom. After untying her and removing her gag, she told me that Em was being held in the master bedroom.

I've never been so scared in my entire life. Not knowing what I was going to see in that bedroom. It was simultaneously better and worse than what my imagination conjured up.

Ember was alive, but a naked man was on top of her, and her body was bloody and battered. I didn't think after that. I couldn't. I reacted like any man would, needing to kill the motherfucker who hurt her.

Little did I know, it'd be my mother who would

have that honor. No matter… he's dead and can't hurt either of them ever again.

Crow also reassured me when he told me that Miguel Cruz and his two sidekicks were dead, and that Journey, Poker, Screamer, and Python were out tracking down the rest of the dealers Cruz gave up just before drawing his last breath.

The threat is gone, to the club, and to my family. All that remains is the threat to my sanity while I watch and wait for Ember to recover.

And to give you an answer to your proposal.

"She's going to say yes."

I whip my head around and stare at my mom. "How can you be so sure?"

"Because she loves you," she says simply. "The time wasn't right before, but it is now."

My throat clogs. "Mom, I thought…"

"Come here, sweetheart."

I look at Ember, ensuring myself that she's still sleeping, and move to sit in the chair next to my mom's bed.

"I know what you thought," she tells me. "You thought the worst, and honestly, short of us both being dead, I'm not sure it could've gotten much worse. But it didn't. We're both here, and so are you. Hold on to that."

"I'm trying."

"Now, I've only got one question for you."

"What's that?"

"Does she make you happy?"

I nod. "Unbelievably happy."

"Then stop worrying. All will work out as it it's meant to."

After imparting that bit of wisdom, she shoos me away, saying she wants to get some sleep. Time passes in a blur. Jackyl brings me clothes, Addison and Wren come in to check on all of us, Poker brings food. The world around me continues to spin while I'm stuck, frozen in place as long as Ember's eyes remain closed.

I rest my head on the bed next to her, and I must doze off because I jolt awake when something touches my hand.

"Parker?"

"Em!" I exclaim, grabbing her hand without thinking. I withdraw when she winces at the contact. "I'm sorry. I didn't mean to hurt you. I just… Fuck, you're awake."

She tries to smile, but her face is swollen and bruised. "Thirsty," she croaks.

I turn around to grab a bottle of water on the stand next to the bed and hand it to her. She needs help to take a few sips, and I gladly oblige. I'd do anything for her.

"How are you feeling?" I ask after returning the water to the table.

"Like I've been hit by a Mack truck."

I cringe at her description. "I'm so sorry I didn't get there sooner."

"But you got there. We're all alive. That's all that matters."

"It never should've gotten that far."

"Stop it," she sasses. "Let it go, please. Because if you don't, I won't be able to." I open my mouth to reply, but she adds, "I'm so tired."

I lean forward and kiss her lips gently. "Get some rest, Em. I'm not going anywhere."

"Promise?"

"I promise."

"Mmm." She licks her lips. "Parker?"

"Yeah?"

"I'll marry you."

EPILOGUE
EMBER

For better or worse.

Six months later...

"I can't believe this still fits."

I grin at Lori in the mirror. Ghost and I are getting married today, and I was determined to wear the dress I had picked out for our original ceremony. Some think it's bad luck, but after mentioning it to Ghost, we agreed that it linked a part of our past with our present. It's all those decisions, good and bad, that led us to where we are now. I couldn't ignore that even if I wanted to.

"It helped that I wasn't feeling myself for two months," I remind her. "I guess that's one good thing that came of that whole mess."

My best friend knows what happened to me, but

she has no idea how it links to the club, and that's the way it's going to stay. Club business is not my business to tell, and I'm fine with that. But there was no way I could hide my injuries from her.

"God, don't even bring that up," she says with a sigh. "No bad juju on your wedding day."

"You're right," I agree. "Only positive thoughts today."

The door opens, and Addison pokes her head in. "You ready?"

"Almost."

"Okay. Mama is starting to get restless, so Ghost wanted me to check," she explains, referring to Mrs. West.

She started insisting that everyone call her Mama, and we do to make things as easy on her as possible. The night of the attack was her truly last good day with the disease she's fighting. She woke up the next morning, confused about where she was, and why Ghost was being nice to me.

We've made peace, her and me, but I had to treat it like a brand-new connection, like there was no history there for her to be angry about. I don't care though. I love her and will do whatever I have to in order to keep her smiling.

"I'm coming now," I say, knowing that there's

little time if Mama's restless. Once that starts, it's hard to calm her down.

"I'm so glad you chose to get married here," Lori says.

"Me, too."

The backyard at Mama's house—our house now as well—is the perfect location for a wedding. It's where Ghost swept me off my feet this time around, and it makes the most sense for Mama.

We turned the basement into a mini apartment so we'd have privacy, but we can't leave Mama. A nursing home is out of the question. We love her too much to pass her off on someone else. It'd be different if I didn't have the knowledge and experience to provide appropriate care, but I do so here we are.

Two minutes later, I'm walking down the makeshift aisle, but Ghost isn't standing at the end of it. I scan the yard, panicking, and then my eyes land on him, easing the pressure in my chest. He's sitting in a chair next to Mama, holding her hand and murmuring something to her. He might be talking to her, but he's looking at me, and all I see in those incredible eyes is love.

I smile to reassure him that it's okay that he's sitting, and to drive the point home, I sit down in the chair on her other side, gripping both of their hands in mine as I do.

The ceremony, while nowhere near conventional, is perfect. We're pronounced man and wife, and he leans past his mom to kiss me softly on the lips when it ends.

The two of us take the time to help Mama inside and get her settled for the night before we return to our guests and enjoy the reception. Anna is going to stay inside with her to make sure she needs or wants for nothing while we're occupied. Mama has become attached to Anna, which has helped immensely when Ghost and I need time to ourselves.

We don't take it often, but we do take it.

"I love you, Mrs. West," Ghost says after closing the bedroom door.

"I love you, too, Mr. West," I reply.

"I'm sorry today didn't go as planned."

I rest my palm on his cheek. "Today was perfect. I wouldn't change a single second of it."

"No?"

"I'm married to you, aren't I?" I counter.

"For better or worse," he teases.

"And it will always be better. Always."

NEXT IN SOULLESS KINGS MC: MARBLE FALLS, TX

BOOK 4: POKER

Cover and blurb coming soon!

IF YOU WANT TO KNOW HOW GHOST FIRST CAME TO BE A SOULLESS KING, YOU CAN DO THAT HERE...

Gibson

Soulless Kings MC: Book #8

Can be read as a standalone, although why not read the entire series?😉**

Gibson: https://books2read.com/GibsonSoullessKings

Gibson...

As a former military medic and the doc for the Soulless Kings MC, I've seen a lot. More than most ER doctors for sure. And treating the Bangin' Betties comes with the territory. They don't exactly live clean lives, but it's not my place to judge. And what they do outside of the clubhouse isn't my business... until it is.

When one of the Bangin' Betties shows up on my doorstep in the middle of the night, beaten and barely clinging to life, I fall back on my training. I don't think, I just act. In doing so, I open up a world of chaos I wasn't prepared for. I don't know what's worse: the mayhem that ensues or the fact that my heart doesn't seem to care that I'm falling in love with the woman who caused it.

Alena...

Whore. Prostitute. Slut. It doesn't matter what people call me as long as I get paid at the end of the night. Unless I'm at the Soulless Kings clubhouse. There I'm a Bangin' Betty and I don't charge. Because they may be wild, but they treat the Betties with respect. I'm not a commodity to them, and realizing I'm worth more than fifty bucks for a back-alley blowjob, I decide to make a change.

Unfortunately, I'm my pimp's highest earner, which isn't saying much. When he tries to *convince* me to stay, I know I only have one option: Soulless Kings MC. By some miracle, I made it to the club's property and their doc's house. But now that he's fixed me up, I realize I have an entirely different problem.

Did I just leave one pimp behind only to be used by the very people I thought I could trust? Or, for the first time in my life, should I trust my gut and give the doc and the Kings a chance?

CHAPTER 1

Gibson

I like to fuck as much as any red-blooded man, but Bangin' Betties are a tricky conquest.

Smoke fills the room, causing a cloudy haze to blanket everyone. The smell of cigars, cigarettes, and marijuana is thick, and it's mixed with the stench of booze and sweat. Classic rock music spills from the speakers in what can only be described as loud, almost bordering on obnoxious. But that's nothing new. This is, after all, a Soulless Kings MC party. It would feel like a run of the mill frat party if there weren't half naked Bangin' Betties walking around or one-time couples fucking on the few couches spread throughout the space.

This is a far cry from your military days.

"Ya gonna stand here all night and gawk, or are you gonna join in on the fun?"

I swivel to look at Fender, my president, who's holding a glass of amber liquor in one hand and a half smoked joint in the other. He's comfortable in this atmosphere, at home. But for those of us who know him well, we know he would be just as comfortable at home on the couch with his ol' lady, Charlie, or in the middle of a war zone holding an assault rifle and shooting at his enemies.

"Do you have any idea how many Betties I've looked at tonight?" I ask in response.

"As a brother, or as a doc?" He chuckles. "Because there's a huge difference."

"You're damn right there's a difference." I snag the joint from his fingers and take a hit. When I exhale, I feel cleansed. Or most of me does. My memory though… that's another story. "I've treated six. Which means I've laid eyes on three twats with varying *ailments*, two mouths lined with cold sores, one infected nipple piercing, and one hand with fingers covered in what can only be described as…" I shudder. "… horrifically gross."

"All in all, not a bad night," Fender jokes, although I fail to see the humor.

"That's a real low bar, Prez."

"Maybe, but it's all part of the territory, Gib. If you'll recall, I gave you the option of not being in charge of the Betties' care."

"You did," I concede. "But I also remember you drilling into me how them seeing a doctor outside of the club could bring a mountain of questions to our door."

"True."

We stand there in silence, observing the party. I instructed those I treated tonight to stay away from anything beyond dancing so nothing gets passed to an unsuspecting horndog, and so far, they all seem to be heading my words.

Fender walks away when he sees Charlie, his ol' lady, extricating herself from a group of women, leaving me to scan the crowd. My eyes land on the door to the clubhouse just as another Betty walks in. *Alena*. Now she's a Bangin' Betty I'd like to examine. She's sinfully sexy in her short skirt and the lacy number some would call a shirt. It leaves nothing to the imagination, but I imagine that comes in real handy at work. She is a prostitute after all.

Alena and I have talked a few times, enjoyed a drink or two together, but we've never crossed that line from friends to lovers. I'd give my left nut to, but she's been around one too many blocks... although, I could easily be persuaded to forget that little bit of info. I also get the impression that she doesn't get enough human interaction that isn't built on sex, so I try to keep that in mind when I'm around her.

I wave my hand in the air to call her over and watch the rhythmic dance of her hips as she walks. The closer she gets, the more her face lights up. Her smile is wide, her white teeth flashing in the minimal lighting. She certainly hasn't let her years working on the street impact her looks.

"I've been waiting for you to ask me to dance all night."

I lower my stare to my arm, glaring at the red-tipped fingernails trailing down my skin. They might as well be razorblades, for all the effect they have on me. I lift my eyes to Dana, another Bangin' Betty. Her smile is just as wide as Alena's, but it's dull, forced... fake as fuck.

I shift my eyes back to Alena, only to see she changed directions and is now being coaxed into a dance by a new hang around, Garret. Anger at the untimely flirting simmers beneath the surface.

Grabbing Dana by the wrist, I remove her hand from my arm and take a step back.

"We've been down this road," I remind her. "We don't mix well."

In other words, she's not the best lay I've ever had, and I've no interest in an encore. Dana is too strung out for my tastes. Sure, she gets the job done, but barely. And when I looked at her in the fresh light of day the next morning, I felt like I needed a giant dose of penicillin.

Don't get me wrong, I like to fuck as much as any red-blooded man, but Bangin' Betties are a tricky conquest. A person can only treat a pussy so much as a doctor before it becomes damn near impossible to get turned on by it.

That's the beauty of Alena… her pimp handles all his girls' medical care. And because he does, they're some of the best out there. Or so I've heard.

"Aw, Gibby, c'mon," Dana prods with a sultry undertone. She's the only one who calls me that, other than my mother, and it makes me cringe. "Gimme another shot. I know we can be good together."

She flattens her palms against my chest and leans her head back. A laugh crawls up the back of my throat at the way her bottom lip is poked out. I know she's trying to look sexy, but she just looks desperate and pathetic. When her arms go around my neck and her fingers through my hair, I once again grab her wrists, a little more forcefully this time.

"Listen, Dana, there are plenty of other guys here." I peel her off of me and push her back a step until my arms lock and she's not able to work her way forward. "You and me… we're not happening again."

For a split second, I think I see rage flash across her face, but it's gone so quickly, replaced by a sultry smile, that I figure I'm imagining things.

"Your loss, Gibby."

With that, she walks away, and the sway of her hips has nothing on Alena.

Speaking of, I flick my gaze in her direction and see Garret with his arms around her waist and his hands draped over her ass. Their bodies are as close as two humans can be without actually fucking right here in front of everyone. Heat sears me from the inside out, red-hot jealousy making itself known. I have no claim on her, so the rush of emotion makes no sense.

I debate on interrupting their foreplay, but before I can, Alena freezes. She steps back from Garret and shoves her hand down her skirt, only to pull out a cell phone. I watch as she taps the screen, the light from it illuminating her face. Her eyes narrow as she, I assume, reads a text message. She taps out a quick reply before saying something to Garret and then kissing him on the cheek and bolting toward the door.

Once she's gone, I stroll in Garret's direction. By the time I reach him, he's already entwined with Sass, one of the Betties I treated earlier.

"Proceed with caution, Garret," I say, loudly enough to be heard over the music.

Sass, short for Sassafras—what were her parents thinking?—glares at me, clearly pissed that I'm interrupting what was sure to end in a quick fuck. Too damn bad. I know what awaits Garret if he continues down this particular road, and I'm not in the mood to treat him too.

Thinking he's in trouble, Garret steps away from Sass and turns to face me. "I'm sorry, Gibson, I didn't realize she was taken."

I chuckle. "She's not. Not by me anyway."

Confusion rolls over his features. I know the moment he finally gets my warning because his eyes widen.

"Oh, right." He looks at Sass. "Sorry, honey, but… maybe next time?"

"Sure, whatever." Sass stomps away and joins Dana and a few other Bangin' Betties on the opposite side of the room.

"Thanks, man," Garret says. "Appreciate it."

"Why'd Alena bolt so fast?" I ask, not giving two shits about his appreciation.

Garret shakes his head, seemingly thrown off by the quick change in topic, but he recovers.

"She said she got called into work."

"Ah, okay."

It makes sense. She's been called away by her pimp before. But it doesn't happen often. Satisfied that nothing was wrong, I leave Garret to return to the bar.

I spend the next hour getting good and drunk so maybe, just maybe, I can go home with a woman tonight… one who can satisfy the itch I have for someone else.

ALSO BY ANDI RHODES

Broken Rebel Brotherhood

Broken Souls

Broken Innocence

Broken Boundaries

Broken Rebel Brotherhood: Next Generation

Broken Hearts

Broken Wings

Broken Mind

Bastards and Badges

Stark Revenge

Slade's Fall

Jett's Guard

Soulless Kings MC

Fender

Joker

Piston

Greaser

Riker

Trainwreck

Squirrel

Gibson

Flash

Royal

Satan's Legacy MC

Snow's Angel

Toga's Demons

Magic's Torment

Duck's Salvation

Dip's Flame

Devil's Handmaidens MC

Harlow's Gamble

Peppermint's Twist

Mama's Rules

Valhalla Rising MC

Viking

Inferno

Reaper

Mayhem Makers

Forever Savage

Saints Purgatory MC

Unholy Soul

Wrathful Malice

Grim's Hell

Shadowy Abyss

Rogue's Cross

Thorn's Vengeance

Spike's Perdition

Soulless Kings MC: Marble Falls, TX

Crow

Journey

ABOUT THE AUTHOR

Andi Rhodes is an author whose passion is creating romance from chaos in all her books! She writes MC (motorcycle club) romance with a generous helping of suspense and doesn't shy away from the more difficult topics. Her books can be triggering for some so consider yourself warned. Andi also ensures each book ends with the couple getting their HEA! Most importantly, Andi is living her real life HEA with her husband and their boxers.

Printed in Great Britain
by Amazon